Sweet Hide and Seek

A SWEET COVE, MASSACHUSETTS

COZY MYSTERY

BOOK 9

J.A. WHITING

D1377771

To hear about new books and book sales, please sign up for my mailing list at: www.jawhitingbooks.com

For my family and friends, with love

CHAPTER 1

Carrying their suitcases as dusk gathered and snowflakes dusted the shoulders of their coats, the four Roseland sisters, followed by their two cats, Euclid and Circe, walked up the steps to the Victorian's front porch and entered the elegant foyer where they plopped their bags on the floor. They had just returned from a mini-vacation at a ski resort with their boyfriends, Mr. Finch and Betty Hayes. The young people skied, snowboarded, and snow-tubed while Finch and Betty took walks, shopped, and sat in comfy chairs reading in front of the roaring fire with two fine felines curled on their laps.

"That vacation was just what I needed." Courtney, the youngest sister, removed her coat and hung it in the entryway closet.

"It was great being outside all day long." Ellie chuckled. "It made me dislike winter less."

Jenna lugged her bag up the carved wooden staircase. "We need to get away more often."

1

The big house felt chilly from having the heat turned down for so many days and Angie went to turn the thermostat up. "When will the next round of bed and breakfast guests be arriving?"

Ellie ran a B and B out of the Victorian mansion that the sisters lived in together. "Early this evening."

Angie's mouth dropped. "That soon?"

Ellie pulled her long hair up into a bun. "We're home, so it's back to business." The tall blonde yawned as she bent to carry her suitcase up the steps. "I probably should have waited until tomorrow to start accepting reservations. If I don't come out of my room in an hour, come and wake me."

Angie had enjoyed the trip immensely as she and her boyfriend were finally able to spend time together focused on each another. Thinking of Josh made Angie's knees weak and a little smile played over her lips. Josh Williams was a businessman and entrepreneur who had recently bought-out his older brother's share in the Sweet Cove Resort in order to run his businesses and his life according to his own wishes, and part of those wishes included living in town close to Angie.

The cats followed Angie through the downstairs rooms of the house as she checked that everything was as it should be and nothing had gone awry while the family had been on their trip. Walking through the living room, the beauty of the space's comfortable, elegant furnishings warmed her heart. Even though it had been a wonderful, fun-filled trip, it was always nice to be home.

Angie looked to the side table in the foyer where they kept the framed photograph of Professor Marion Linden, the woman who left the Victorian mansion to Angie when she passed away. The sisters later discovered that Professor Linden was their great aunt.

Just as Angie smiled at the photo and mouthed *thank you for our lovely home* to the image of the professor, Euclid, the huge orange Maine Coon cat jumped up onto the side table set in front of the big windows that looked out onto the front porch. He flicked his plume of a tail slowly back and forth. Circe, the delicate black cat with a white patch on her chest, sat on the area rug at the base of the table and watched her feline friend.

Something about what the cats were doing sent a shiver down Angie's back and she pulled her cardigan tight around herself. As she walked into the sunroom that was off the living room, she put her forefinger against the soil of the plant pots to check if they needed watering, glanced out the window to the backyard, and then returned to the living room. Euclid still stared out the window and Circe sat quietly on the floor as if she was waiting for something. Standing at the edge of the living room watching the cats, Angie felt a sense of unease grip her stomach.

"What's cookin,' Sis?" Courtney came into the room from the foyer. "You see a ghost or something?"

Angie pointed at the cats and Courtney turned her attention to the two sentinels. "Are they waiting for something?"

Angie made eye contact with her sister.

Courtney grinned. "You're kidding. Really? We just got home. Something's happening already? Cool." She was the one sister who loved figuring out the clues and suspects of a mystery. She and Mr. Finch enjoyed watching crime shows together and they both claimed to learn a good deal from the episodes, which came in handy when they were sometimes called in to help the town police chief with difficult cases. The Roseland sisters and Mr. Finch often "consulted" for the Sweet Cove Police Department because they each had a special skill ... and those skills fell under the category of paranormal powers.

"I'm starting to feel anxious." Angie frowned. "Do you feel anything?"

Courtney sat down on the sofa and looked at the two animals. She closed her eyes for a minute trying to pick up on anything floating on the air. Suddenly, her eyes popped open and she stood up. "I need something to eat." She headed for the kitchen.

"You didn't feel anything?" Angie followed after her sister with a puzzled look on her face.

"Oh, I did. Something's brewing alright and it's going to show up soon." Courtney looked over her shoulder with a smile. "I want to eat a sandwich while I have a chance."

Angie glanced back to the cats. They sat like statues in the same spots, unmoving. Angie frowned. The cats hadn't budged even though Courtney had mentioned food.

It wasn't a good sign.

***

Courtney removed frozen pea soup from the freezer and defrosted it in the microwave while Angie prepared sandwiches of goat cheese, pesto, and sun-dried tomatoes. She removed the panini press from one of the lower cabinets, brushed one side of each sandwich with olive oil, and placed them, one at a time, into the press for grilling. Courtney poured the defrosted soup into a pot and warmed it on the stove.

"So," Courtney said as she removed bowls and plates from the shelves and cabinets. "What do you think is about to happen?"

Angie raised an eyebrow. "Something that needs our attention."

Courtney stirred the soup. "When I sat on the sofa, I felt that something wasn't right. I felt a sense that things were out of order."

"With us? With our family?" Angie's brow

creased with worry.

"No, it had to do with someone outside the family."

The back door opened and after wiping his feet on the mat, Mr. Finch came into the kitchen. "I have unpacked and put things away." He rested his cane against the wall while he removed his winter coat. Finch lived in the house directly behind the Roseland's Victorian and as an adopted member of the family, he was a welcome fixture in their home, anytime, day or night.

"Where's Betty?" Angie asked.

"She has returned to her own house to do laundry and take a nap." Finch walked slowly into the room and sat down at the kitchen island.

"A nap? Betty?" Angie was incredulous. Betty Hayes, a successful Sweet Cove Realtor, was like a force of nature, energetic and always in constant motion.

"Miss Betty enjoyed the rest and relaxation of the trip." Finch smiled. "I teased her that she might decide to retire soon."

Courtney made a harrumphing sound. "That woman will never retire."

"I believe you are correct, Miss Courtney."

"Would you like a sandwich?" Angie asked Finch.

"It smells delicious." Finch took a deep breath. "I would love a sandwich."

While the girls finished preparing the early

6

evening meal, Finch glanced up to the refrigerator. "Where are the cats?"

Angie stopped working. "They're keeping watch at the living room window."

"Are they? Already?" Finch made eye contact with Angie. "I am not surprised."

"You feel something, too, Mr. Finch?" Courtney carried a bowl of soup over to the island and placed it in front of the older man who lifted his spoon and dipped it into the steaming liquid.

Finch looked over the rims of his black framed glasses. "Indeed, I do."

"Courtney and I sense something, but we don't have a clear idea of what it's about." Angie removed a sandwich from the panini grill. "I'd hoped things would stay quiet for a while ... but that never happens." She brought the sandwiches to Courtney and Mr. Finch. "Do you have any sense of what it's going to involve?"

Mr. Finch was thoughtful for a few moments. "The sensation is vague and unformed, but I feel sadness, loss, a longing for something that is no more, or perhaps, never was."

Angie looked at the man. "Could the feelings be left over from the last case we helped with recently?"

Finch slowly shook his head. "These feelings are fresh ... at least, where we are concerned."

Angie returned to the panini press for the last sandwich. "I haven't gotten over that last case."

The Roseland sisters and Mr. Finch had helped with a case involving a missing young man, who had been killed by a friend of his who had been enraged with jealousy.

Mr. Finch gave a slight nod of agreement. "That was a terrible loss under very sad circumstances."

Angie carried her plate to the kitchen island and sat on the stool next to her youngest sister. "Let's talk about more pleasant things. I want to hold on just a little longer to the happy feelings we had on our vacation." Thoughts of the fun she'd had with her family, friends, and Josh Williams danced around in Angie's mind and sent a flood of warmth through her heart.

"Right." Courtney used her spoon to stir the piping hot pea soup in her bowl. "Trouble knows where to find us and it will find us soon enough. Let's eat."

Just as they were raising the sandwiches to their mouths, the doorbell rang.

Courtney sighed. "Couldn't it have given us just ten more minutes so we could eat?"

CHAPTER 2

Finch, Angie, and Courtney groaned in unison.

Angie put her untouched sandwich back on her plate. "Shall I go?"

"What about Ellie?" Courtney's voice was hopeful. "Maybe it's a B and B guest. She'll go."

"Ellie's still napping." Angie slid off the stool.

"I think the three of us should go." Mr. Finch removed his cane from the overhang of the countertop.

The three made their way down the hall to the front door where they saw the cats sitting at attention in the foyer waiting for someone to open the door.

"They don't look alarmed." Courtney whispered, eyeing the two felines.

Angie opened the door to find an older woman who was probably in her late-sixties standing on the porch holding the handle of a rolling suitcase. The woman wore a black woolen winter coat and had a head full of short, dark auburn curls that framed her face. Bright hazel eyes looked at Angie expectantly. "Hello. Are you Ellie Roseland?"

"Come in." Angie stepped back and opened the door wider to allow the woman to enter. "Ellie's upstairs. I'm her sister, Angie." Courtney and Finch were introduced. "We'll help you get settled."

"What a gorgeous place." The woman's eyes took in the beauty of the furnishings, the carved wooden staircase, the gleaming hardwood floors, and the antique area rug that was placed under the polished, round table in the middle of the foyer. The woman rested her hand against her cheek. "My. It's heavenly."

"Would you care for some hot tea or coffee?" Mr. Finch asked. "The evening refreshments haven't been put out yet."

"I'd love a cup of tea." The woman stood her suitcase upright and removed her coat.

Courtney took the coat from her and hung it in the closet. "May I ask your name? I'll go look up your reservation and get your room key and the registration forms."

"Orla O'Brien. Pleased to meet all of you." The woman smiled. "I'm exhausted. Traveling can be such a draining experience."

Mr. Finch gestured to the dining room. "Would you like to sit down? I'll have your tea in a moment."

"We also have some pea soup and homemade bread." Courtney called over her shoulder as she headed down the hall to the office.

"Wonderful." Before taking a seat, Orla walked around the dining room brushing her hand over the top of the long table and gazing at the dishes and goblets in the China cabinet. Circe and Euclid kept their eyes on the woman and followed her into the dining room while keeping their distance. Angie watched them for any reaction they might have towards the new guest.

"Have you come to Sweet Cove from far away?" Angie asked.

Orla bent slightly and peered into the China cabinet. "I've been traveling for years. I enjoy seeing new places, meeting new people. My permanent home is in California." She rubbed her lower back. "I fear all this traveling is playing havoc with my back though, too much sitting on trains and planes."

Finch carried in a small tray with a pot of tea, a cup and saucer, a little jug of cream, and a sugar bowl. He placed it on the table and Orla let out a sigh of gratitude before taking a seat.

"Just what I needed." The woman poured the hot liquid into her cup, added cream, but no sugar, and sipped. "I've never been to New England in the winter." A tinkling chuckle slipped from her lips. "I believe this bitter cold weather explains why I haven't."

"The cold here can be brutal." Angie agreed. "It's much nicer to visit during one of the other seasons."

Mr. Finch sat down across from Orla. "But winter has its own beauty. If you bundle up against the cold, you can take in some lovely sights. The sea is often wild and dramatic in winter and there are the museums and art galleries to visit. The bonus is there are no crowds at this time of year."

Orla gave Finch a warm smile. "What a lovely attitude." Nodding, she added, "I have many things on my list to see."

Euclid and Circe leapt up to the China cabinet and their sudden movement startled Orla who gasped and placed her hand on her ample chest. "Oh. You have cats. I didn't notice them when I came in."

"The fine orange boy is Euclid." Mr. Finch smiled up at them. "And the lovely black cat is called Circe."

"Ah, the goddess of magic." Orla made eye contact with the two animals.

Angie sat down at the table next to Orla and looked up to see the cats gazing down on the woman without any emotion. Angie wanted to let out a sigh of relief that the felines didn't object to the newly-arrived guest. Not yet anyway.

"You know mythology," Mr. Finch observed.

"Some." Orla lifted her cup to her lips.

"What did you do for work, Ms. O'Brien?" Finch asked amiably.

"Oh, my. Many jobs. I didn't have one career. I taught French and Spanish for many years. I draw

12

in pastels and sell some of my work in galleries."

"How fascinating." Mr. Finch told the woman. Mr. Finch loved art, collected a few pieces, and enjoyed sketching and painting.

Courtney entered the room carrying a tray with another pot of tea and some cups, a tureen of the soup, a bowl, and a bread basket. She placed a bottle of olive oil on the table for dipping the bread.

Removing a key and some reservation forms from her sweater pocket, she put them beside Orla's place setting and indicated where the woman needed to fill in the information. Orla reached into the purse at her feet and took out a wallet. While Courtney busied herself taking things from the tray and putting them onto the table, Orla opened her wallet to get her license and credit card.

Angie idly watched Orla's fingers slipping the cards from the holders. A third card dropped to the tabletop and Orla scooped it up and put it back in the wallet ... but not before Angie spotted something.

A tingle caused the little blonde hairs on Angie's arms to stand up.

Mr. Finch poured three cups of tea, one for Courtney, one for Angie, and one for himself. As he passed them around the table, footsteps could be heard on the staircase, and Ellie came into the dining room. "I apologize for not being here to welcome you." Ellie stopped suddenly and stared at the woman at the dining table for a few beats, and then she shook herself and walked closer so she could extend her hand to shake with the new guest as she introduced herself.

The doorbell rang and Ellie went to answer it. An older man who looked to be in his early seventies entered the foyer, shaking a bit of snow from his shoulders. The cats leapt down from the cabinet and raced into the foyer where they sat on the steps in the middle of the staircase to observe the new guest.

"Bitter cold," the very large, heavy, bald man sputtered. "I don't know why I travel in the winter. I'm Mel Abel." The bald man introduced himself in a loud voice as he rubbed his hands up and down his arms. "It's frigid out there." He looked at Ellie with clear blue eyes and a slight smile. "I could use a hot drink. A hot toddy would do the trick." The man folded his coat and placed it over the top of his suitcase.

Mr. Finch rose from his seat at the dining table. "I would be happy to prepare some hot toddies. Who would like one?"

The new guest shot his hand into the air just as Orla raised hers.

"Off I go. Back in a flash." Finch took his cane and headed for the kitchen to make the warm drinks.

Courtney started for the office for the keys and reservation forms when the front doorbell rang again causing her to glance back over her shoulder.

"You're kidding me," she muttered.

Angie opened the door this time. A petite, slender woman in her early to mid-forties entered the Victorian. "I have a reservation, but I wondered if I could keep my departure date open-ended as I'm unsure how long I'm going to stay. Do you have a vacant room that might be open for at least a week?" Since people were arriving like waves upon the shore, Angie looked to Ellie for an answer.

Ellie nodded. "Yes, we have a room you can have for the week. We can probably accommodate you for an even longer visit, if necessary."

The short woman wore her light brown hair in a chin-length bob. She told Angie her name. "Cora Connors. I'm most grateful." The new arrival's coat seemed too thin for the weather and she carried a worn, battered duffel bag. A look of weariness pulled at the woman's shoulders and at the corners of her mouth. Angie imagined that a great weight had settled over Ms. Connors causing her a heavy sense of fatigue.

"May I?" Cora pointed at the dining room.

"Yes, please. We'll bring in some more drinks and snacks." Angie turned for the kitchen just as Courtney came into the dining room from the office carrying keys and forms. When she noticed Cora, her eyebrows shot up. "Oh. Another guest." Courtney went back down the hall to get more forms.

Angie took a look at the cats as she left the foyer.

Euclid had a scowl on his face as his head swiveled from new guest to new guest. Circe sat beside him on the step gazing at the new people in the house. Angie caught their eyes and gave a little shrug. Entering the kitchen, she met Mr. Finch who was busying himself making the hot drinks.

"The new guests seem pleasant enough." Finch took glasses from the cabinet. "Perhaps trouble will pass us by today."

"Maybe." Angie arranged some cookies on a platter. "Except for one thing."

Finch faced the young woman with a questioning expression.

"When Orla O'Brien took out her credit card, another card slipped onto the table. She picked it up and shoved it back in its place."

"So?" Finch cocked his head.

"It was a driver's license. With Orla's picture on it."

Finch waited.

"Only the name on the license was *not* Orla O'Brien."

CHAPTER 3

"Are you sure it was our guest who was in the license photo?" Finch pondered. "Perhaps it was her sister or someone else in her family who looks just like her?"

"It was definitely Orla." Angie was sure of it.

"Most interesting." Mr. Finch's bushy gray eyebrows squeezed together. "Why would she have two licenses with different names?"

"I can't come up with a good reason." Angie folded her arms over her chest.

"I can see that she might have changed her last name due to marriage or what not." Finch arranged the drinking glasses on the wheeled beverage cart. "But why would she change her first name as well?"

"It doesn't make any sense." Angie pushed the cart towards the hallway. "Keep your eyes on her, Mr. Finch."

"Where are the cats?" Finch looked about to see if the animals had come into the kitchen.

"They're at the front of the house with the guests

listening to every word they utter."

Before Angie and Finch reached the dining room with the drink cart, they could hear the amiable chatter of the people sitting around the large table. Angie placed the hot drinks in front of Orla and Mel. Finch carried his glass to the table and sat down. Cora sat meekly at the far end of the table clutching a mug of tea and listening to the two other guests discuss their travels to different parts of the world.

Angie chose the seat next to the woman and started a conversation with her. "Do you travel much?"

Cora seemed slightly startled to have been spoken to and she looked at Angie with wide, dark brown eyes. "Me? Oh, no. I haven't had the opportunity to do things like that." She took a swallow of tea. "Though I would love to."

"Maybe one day." Angie smiled. "What brings you to Sweet Cove?"

Cora's fingers seemed to shake slightly when she let go of her mug. "A friend and I were going to meet for a few days and stay at several bed and breakfast inns along the coast. We hadn't seen each other in a long while. Her plans changed and she couldn't make it, but I decided to come anyway." The woman gave a shrug of her shoulder.

"Are there things in particular you'd like to see?"

"I want to visit Salem and the Witch Museum." Cora accepted a bowl of soup from Courtney. "I'm not sure what's around here to see."

When Cora mentioned the Witch Museum, even though Orla was deep in conversation with Mr. Abel, she flashed the woman an odd look. For a moment, Angie caught Orla's gaze and when the two made eye contact, a shiver ran through Angie's blood, unnerving her.

Angie turned to Cora. "Ellie has lots of brochures on the historical sites, the museums, and the shops in the Sweet Cove area. She can help you plan your visit."

"I'll ask her for suggestions." Cora nodded and dipped her spoon into the pea soup. "Wonderful soup. So flavorful."

Mel Abel turned his big, pumpkin-like face to Cora and Angie. "Why so quiet down that end of the table? Nothing to contribute to our conversation?"

Cora lifted her eyes to Mel for just a moment, and then quickly looked back to her soup not replying to the man.

"We'd be happy to join in." Angie deflected the attention away from Cora. "What are you talking about?"

"Politics and religion." Mel let out a belly laugh. "The two topics that no one should ever discuss." He smiled. "In fact," we are *not* talking about those subjects. I like to pull people's legs. We're talking about traveling."

Angie asked, "Where is everyone's favorite place

19

that they've been to visit?"

The question started a round of discussion about where people had enjoyed visiting. Mel spoke first in his booming voice. "My favorite trip was to New Zealand. Can't beat the scenery." The man winked. "And Paris, too. Loved the shopping."

"How about you, Ms. O'Brien?" Finch asked. "Do you have a favorite place that you've visited?'

Orla gave Finch a nod. "Ireland. When I'm there, I can feel the spirits of my ancestors rising in the mists and in the beauty of the landscape."

"Well said." Finch smiled.

Even though Orla had voiced a lovely sentiment, her words seemed to pinch at Angie's skin. The ring of the front doorbell caused Angie to nearly jump out of her seat and to cover her anxiousness, she stood up. "I'll get it."

Opening the door, she was surprised to see Jack Ford standing in the glow of the porch light. Snowflakes were sprinkled over the shoulders of his black woolen coat and his navy blue bowtie peeked out at the neck.

Angie blinked. "Jack. I didn't know you were coming."

Jack entered the foyer, rested his briefcase on the floor, removed his coat, and nodded to the people at the dining table as Ellie rushed over to her boyfriend. "Is everything okay? I wasn't expecting you."

Jack reached for his leather briefcase.

"Everything's fine." He gave Ellie a warm smile and a hug. "I'm meeting a client." Jack, a Sweet Cove lawyer, brushed some snow from his hair.

"A client? Here?" Ellie turned towards the new guests who were all staring into the foyer.

With a blush coloring her cheeks, Cora Connors rose from her seat and walked slowly towards Jack. "It's me. I arranged with Attorney Ford to meet me here." The petite woman shook hands with Jack and introduced herself.

"Oh, well then. Good." Ellie pushed her long blonde hair over her shoulder. "Why don't you take the sunroom. No one is using it. You can close the doors between the sunroom and the living room for privacy." Ellie led them out of the foyer.

When Angie turned around, everyone at the dining table was still staring her way. With her mind racing, wondering why Cora needed to meet Jack, Angie cleared her throat and headed into the dining room. "Can I get anyone anything else? Another drink?" She bustled about clearing away dirty plates and glasses.

Courtney caught her sister's eye and raised an eyebrow.

Mel Abel voiced what the others were thinking. "Why would the woman want to meet with an attorney here? While on vacation?"

Angie smiled, trying to deflect attention away from Cora's and Jack's meeting. "Maybe it was the most convenient time for her."

"What?" Mel snorted. "No lawyers where she's from? It seems fishy to me."

"I'm sure it's all above-board," Mr. Finch said reassuringly. "Perhaps Ms. Connors wanted to speak with Attorney Ford because Jack is an expert in certain areas. She may have traveled to Sweet Cove just to be able to meet with him."

"Still seems fishy." Mel downed the remaining liquid in his glass and set the tumbler on the table with a flourish. "I suppose it's none of our business." He stood up. "I guess I'll head up to my room. I'd love a shower and to change out of these clothes."

Courtney led the man to the second floor guest rooms just as Jenna was coming down the staircase. Introductions were made, Jenna continued down the stairs, and seeing Angie standing in the dining room, she headed that way. "I thought I heard voices down here. I didn't realize that guests had arrived." Jenna spotted Orla O'Brien sitting at the table. "Oh, hi."

Orla smiled warmly. "Hello."

Jenna's eyes widened. The way that Orla looked at her and said hello made Jenna wonder if they'd met before. Angie thought the same thing and spun around to look at Orla with a quizzical expression on her face.

With his tail twitching back and forth, Euclid looked down from the China cabinet with a scowl on his face.

"Have we met?" Jenna stepped further into the room.

Holding Jenna's eyes, Orla shook her head. "No, we haven't."

"Oh." Jenna returned the woman's smile, but Angie could see how stiffly her twin sister held herself. "How long will you be staying in Sweet Cove?"

"I haven't decided that yet." Orla stretched to get the kinks out of her back. "We'll see how things go."

"You're planning some sightseeing?" Jenna didn't know why she felt so uncomfortable in the woman's presence.

"Some." Orla stood up, stretched, and picked up her bag. "I'll head up to my room now. All this traveling makes me tired. Thank you for the soup."

Courtney led Orla O'Brien to the second floor.

Jenna plopped in the chair next to Mr. Finch. "What's this all about?"

Finch and Angie caught Jenna up on the three new B and B guests. "Ms. Connors is meeting with Jack right now in the sunroom."

Angie explained in a hushed voice how Orla had a second license in her purse and that the photo was of Orla, but the name did not match how she'd introduced herself to the family. Euclid let out a low growl.

"Weird." A cloud had settled over Jenna's face. "And she seemed like she knew me. The way she greeted me made me think we'd met before or she knew me from someplace. It made me feel weird."

"That woman makes me feel like I need to be cautious around her." Angie sat, put her elbow on the table, and rested her chin in her hand. "When she talked about Ireland and her ancestors, a strange feeling shot through me. I didn't like it."

Courtney, her honey-blonde hair bouncing around her shoulders, came back downstairs. "What's up with these guests? Sheesh. They're getting odder and odder."

Angie told her sister about the license that fell out of Orla's wallet.

"Huh." Courtney looked off across the room. "What's up with that? Can anyone think of a legitimate reason why someone might have two licenses with two different names?"

Jenna offered an idea. "She works for the government? FBI? CIA?"

"You'd think a government agent would be more careful about having her alternate ID card slip from her wallet." Courtney shook her head. "Maybe she's in a witness protection program?"

Several suggestions were considered and discarded. No one could come up with any ideas that made sense.

"Did you notice what the other name was?" Mr. Finch asked Angie.

Angie frowned recalling the incident. "It happened too fast. I saw the photo and noticed that the name was too long to say Orla O'Brien, so I squinted at it. It looked like Carleen or something like that and the last name was not O'Brien. I'm sure of it."

Courtney leaned forward and used a conspiratorial tone. "Maybe we can get Ellie to check out Orla's wallet when she goes to clean the room tomorrow."

"You know Ellie won't do anything like that. She's made that clear in the past." Angie rubbed her chin. "That would be an invasion of privacy. We'll have to figure out another way to see the other license."

"What do you have in mind, Miss Angie?" Finch asked.

Angie groaned. "I haven't gotten that far yet."

Courtney glanced over her shoulder to the staircase. "We'd better be on guard around these people." She sighed. "It's certainly not how I expected it to show up, but our anticipated trouble may have just arrived at the B and B."

CHAPTER 4

When Jack and Cora Connors emerged from the sunroom, Ellie showed Cora to her room and Jack went into the dining room to join Angie, Mr. Finch, Jenna, and Courtney at the table. The four faces stared at Jack as he took a seat.

Jack looked from one to the next. "You know I can't reveal anything Mrs. Connors talked to me about. Client confidentiality has to be upheld."

Euclid let out a howl from atop the cabinet causing Jack to jump. "Euclid, gee. What's wrong with him?"

Courtney scowled. "He doesn't like people keeping things from us."

"Is everything okay with Mrs. Connors?" Angie questioned. "She seems quiet and worried."

"I can't speak to that." Jack glanced up at Euclid bracing himself for another howl.

Jenna leaned forward and made eye contact with Jack. "Is she in any danger?"

Jack's eyebrows shot up. "Danger? Why would you say that?"

Courtney brought a plate of cookies from the buffet and set them in the center of the table. "Because. Cora Connors shows up at a bed and breakfast inn and wants to speak to a lawyer? It's a tiny bit out of the ordinary." Lifting a cookie from the platter, Courtney bit into it and brandished the remaining part of the cookie in the air. "Something tells me the woman is trying to hide something or maybe she's afraid of something or...."

Mr. Finch looked over the rims of his eyeglasses at Jack. "If Mrs. Connors is in danger, then *we* might be in danger as well. Are you able to warn us if something is amiss?"

Ellie came into the room and put a hand on Jack's shoulder. "Don't badger Jack. As a lawyer, he has certain standards he must hold to. He can't be blabbing confidential information to other people. Imagine being in the client's position. You wouldn't want your private concerns aired to a bunch of people you don't even know." Ellie leaned down and kissed Jack's cheek before taking a seat next to him. "Jack is an honorable man."

Jack blushed and the corners of his mouth turned up.

"We all know Jack." Courtney fussed. "We all know he has integrity and we aren't asking him to compromise that. We *are* asking if Mrs. Connors might be in any danger ... which could result in putting all of us in danger since she's staying here at the inn." She looked from Jack to Ellie.

"Warnings can be on a need-to-know basis. We aren't asking to be told the woman's problems, we're asking if those problems might become *our* problems and if they might compromise a safe environment in our home. That's all we want to know."

"Fine." Ellie stood. "Jack and I are going out for a little while. All the guests I was expecting to arrive have checked in. Things should be quiet. Call me if you need me." Ellie and Jack went to the foyer closet, put on their coats, and headed for the front door.

Courtney whispered to the others with a wicked grin. "We all just got back from vacation, but Ellie and Jack need to go out together again." She formed her fingers into a heart and placed them against her chest.

"I heard that." Ellie opened the front door.

Jack was about to follow Ellie out onto the porch when he hesitated. Turning back to face the people around the table, he said quietly, "You might want to keep your eyes open." Jack headed out of the house with Ellie, leaving Mr. Finch and the three Roseland sisters sitting in the dining room with open mouths. Even Euclid was too surprised to hiss or howl.

"Well. I wasn't expecting that." Jenna leaned back in her chair.

"So we *do* need to be on guard." Courtney nodded. "I knew it."

Mr. Finch spoke. "But, is the danger from Mrs. Connors herself or is she in danger from an outside source?"

"That's a good question." Angie's brow furrowed in worry and confusion as she pushed a strand of her honey-blonde hair out of her eyes.

Courtney's blue eyes brightened. "She could be a fugitive, or what about a witness to an event, or maybe someone is after something she has in her possession. This is getting interesting." Courtney thrived on mystery and adventure and loved that the family members all had special "skills" that often helped the police figure out cases. "Does anyone sense something in particular?"

"Not exactly." Angie sighed. "I feel like things are off and need to be realigned."

"How cryptic." Jenna gave her twin sister a smile. The two girls were fraternal twins, and although they bore a resemblance, they were very different in appearance. Jenna was taller with long dark hair and Angie's hair was the same shade of dark blonde as Courtney's.

Mr. Finch shifted in his seat. "As I told Miss Angie earlier, I feel a sense of loss and sadness over something that is no more."

"Cora does seem to have a sense of sadness about her." Angie thought about the woman. "She seems frail ... emotionally, but not really physically."

"So she probably isn't the danger itself," Jenna

considered. "The danger has to be something she's concerned about. Maybe she feels threatened by something."

"I wonder why she would seek out Jack." Mr. Finch thought about the young lawyer from Sweet Cove. "Her desire to speak with Jack could be a clue to what's going on."

"Good thinking, Mr. Finch." Courtney looked at her sisters. "What are Jack's specialties?"

"Financial stuff, right?" Angie glanced around for confirmation. "Trusts, incorporating businesses, wealth management, things like that."

"He does wills and estate planning, too," Jenna added.

Finch brought up something else. "I believe Jack is also well-versed in identity theft."

"Huh." Angie frowned. "Identity theft. Considering the appearance of the two licenses in Orla O'Brien's wallet, identity theft might be something *she's* involved with, not Cora."

Mr. Finch adjusted his glasses. "An interesting thought."

"Let's keep our focus on Cora right now," Jenna said. "We can get to Orla later."

Angie looked at Courtney. "Did you notice when Cora filled out the form what she wrote down as her permanent residence?"

Courtney stood up. "Back in a second." In less than a minute, the youngest Roseland sister returned to the room carrying Cora's registration form. "It says her place of residence is Mill City, Massachusetts."

"That's in central Massachusetts, about an hour away." Jenna nodded. "That city was an important textile center in the 1800s." She took her phone out and tapped Cora's name and city into the search engine. "I'm looking her up."

"I doubt Cora's current problems will come up in a list on the internet." Courtney sat down again.

Jenna's eyes widened. "What in the world?" She squinted at the phone screen for a half minute, reading, and then she lifted her face to the others. "Listen to this." Jenna read the information from the article out loud, paraphrasing most of it. "Cora's husband, Richard, was a self-employed real estate appraiser and inspector. Early last September, he disappeared."

"What happened to the man?" Finch's eyebrows scrunched together so they looked like one long furry caterpillar sitting over his eyes.

Jenna read some more. "No one knows."

"What were the circumstances?" Angie asked.

"It was a Sunday. Richard Connors went to the town donut shop around 7am, and then returned to his home. He and his twenty-two-year-old son had breakfast together, Richard spent some time answering emails in his office, and then around 11am he went outside to mow the lawn. He stopped mowing to say goodbye to his son who was going out for a few hours. When the son came home, his father wasn't there. That evening, Richard's wife, Cora, returned home from a three-day vacation with her best friend to find that Richard was still not at home. She called the police to report her husband missing." Jenna looked up. "It seems the man was never found. No trace of him. He vanished."

"How very odd." Angie's forehead was lined with concern. "Poor Cora, to never know what happened to her husband. That's awful."

"Maybe the son killed his father," Courtney speculated. "He was the last person to see Richard."

"Does the article say anything else?" Mr. Finch asked.

"It says that the clothes the father was wearing when he mowed the lawn were in the laundry. Also, Richard only wore tan deck shoes. Those were the only kind of shoes he ever wore. His shoes were sitting on the floor of the mud room closet of the house, like Richard removed them after mowing the lawn. Cora and her son noticed that the four pairs of Richard's deck shoes were still in the house, none were missing. Cora is quoted as saying how strange it would be for someone to deliberately take off for somewhere in bare feet." Jenna stopped reading and looked up from her phone to see someone crossing the foyer towards them. Her eyes widened and her face flushed.

Cora Connors stood on the threshold to the

dining room, her hands clasped together in front of her.

When Angie followed Jenna's gaze and saw Cora, she stood up abruptly. "Oh."

Cora shuffled a few steps into the room. "Attorney Ford suggested that I talk to you."

"Us?" Courtney sputtered.

Cora nodded. "He said you might be able to help me."

The sisters and Mr. Finch looked at one another with surprised expressions, each one wondering why Jack would suggest such a thing.

Angie gestured to one of the chairs inviting Cora to join them. "What do you need help with?"

Cora sank into the seat and rested her arms on the tabletop. Sadness and worry seemed to press down on her. She lifted her weary eyes to the people sitting around the table. "Everything."

CHAPTER 5

Stunned to be asked for help and baffled that Jack told Cora to talk to them, no one said anything for a few moments. Even the cats were silent on their perch on the top of the dining room cabinet.

"Why don't I get some tea for all of us and then we can talk." Jenna headed for the kitchen.

"I'm sorry to be a bother." Cora's brown eyes flicked from person to person.

"You're not a bother at all." As soon as the words were spoken, Angie considered that Cora might very well become a bother very soon. She couldn't imagine what circumstances had brought the woman to Sweet Cove and necessitated a meeting with Jack.

"We all need some help from time to time." Mr. Finch reassured her.

"Why did Jack suggest you talk to us?" Courtney asked the question that everyone was thinking.

"Attorney Ford said that you have experience helping the police solve difficult cases." Cora twirled the white gold band on her left ring finger.

Courtney's eyebrows went up and she looked at Finch and Angie with wide eyes. None of them had suspected that Jack knew they often were called in by Police Chief Martin to advise and assist him with certain aspects of investigations. "Huh. I thought we'd hid that fact fairly well from Jack." Courtney gave a weak grin. "I guess not."

Cora's forehead crinkled in confusion, but before she could ask a question, Jenna came in carrying a tray with tea pots, China cups, cream, sugar, linen napkins, and silver spoons.

Once the tea was poured and cups were passed around, Angie spoke. "Would you like to tell us what's troubling you?" she asked with a gentle tone.

Everyone knew that Cora's worries must involve her missing husband ... *if* he was still missing. Jenna only had time to read one article about the man's disappearance before Cora showed up in the dining room. For all they knew, the man had been found ... one way or another.

"I heard you talking about my husband." Cora picked up her cup.

"We...." Angie started to explain.

"It's okay." Cora nodded. "I understand. You wanted to know why I needed to meet with a lawyer. Anyone would be curious." She sipped from her teacup. "I think I should start with my husband's disappearance." Cora seemed to straighten up and push her shoulders back, steeling herself to relive the awful thing that happened only a few months ago.

She began the story. "As you must have read, Richard had a normal Sunday morning that day. Our son, Karl, had recently moved back home. That morning, Richard and Karl had breakfast together, they read the news, talked. Richard had his own appraisal business so he spent some time answering emails and setting up appointments for the coming week. Karl told me that he'd watched a little TV and then took a shower. He was going out to see a friend. On his way to his car, Karl stopped to say goodbye to Richard. Richard was mowing the lawn when Karl left. When Karl came home, his dad wasn't there. Richard's car was in the garage and his wallet and phone were on the kitchen table so Karl assumed his dad went out for a run or a walk."

Jenna asked, "The house was in order? No sign of a struggle?"

Cora moved her head slowly back and forth from side to side. "Everything was the way it always was. Nothing indicated a struggle of any kind."

"Was your husband having trouble with anyone?" Angie questioned. "Had an appraisal gone wrong? Did someone have a grudge or a vendetta against Richard?"

"He never mentioned any such thing." A frown made the skin around the woman's eyes sag. "The police wondered that, as well, if someone was angry with Richard, but they never uncovered anything like that."

"Had your husband ever gone off like this prior to that day?" Finch wondered if this might be a recurring problem.

"Never," Cora said firmly.

Courtney asked, "Did Richard have any trouble with depression or anxiety?"

"No. Richard was easy-going. Most things didn't bother him at all. Even when his work seemed stressful, he would step away from it for an hour to go for a run or read or make a cup of coffee. Richard always said you had to roll with the punches. He wanted to enjoy his life and he was able to manage stress well." Cora looked down at her cup. "Richard was a pleasant person, nice to be around."

"You were on a short vacation with a friend right before Richard went missing?" Angie asked.

"My best friend, Jill, and I went on a long weekend trip every year. We'd been doing that since right after college. We'd go to an inn in a nice little town, walk around, shop, eat out, get a manicure. It was a great time to do girl things together. I always returned home relaxed." Cora hesitated, and then added in a small voice. "Except that one time."

"What about your son?" Jenna set her teacup down. "Was anyone angry with him? Could someone have come to the house to find Karl and ended up having an argument with Richard?"

Cora shook her head. "No one was angry with Karl."

Something pinged in Angie's stomach and she took a quick glance at Courtney who ever so slightly raised an eyebrow.

Euclid stood up on the cabinet, arched his back, and let out a low hiss.

Courtney decided to pursue the angle. "You mentioned that Karl had recently moved back with you and your husband. Had he been in school?"

"Yes. Karl graduated in the spring last year. He did some contract work for a while, but it dried up and he moved home to save some money."

"Is the young man still living at home?" Mr. Finch poured more tea into his cup.

"He is. He just started a part time position. Karl hopes it will lead to full time work eventually."

"What does he do?" Jenna asked.

"Marketing."

"Do you have other children?" Angie leaned forward.

"Richard and I have two sons. Karl is the youngest. Roman is twenty-five." Cora anticipated the next question. "Roman doesn't live at home. He works full-time. He wasn't living at home when Richard went missing."

"Does Roman live in the area?" Mr. Finch held his cane by his side and rubbed the top of it.

"Roman has an apartment in Mill City not far from our house."

Jenna speculated. "The police must have looked into the boys' friends and acquaintances to see if anyone bore a grudge towards any of them?"

"The police checked that out." Cora sighed. "That's part of the puzzling aspects of this case. Richard and the boys got along well with people. They're all nice, friendly men. We can't think of a single person who would wish harm on any of them."

"And *your* friends and acquaintances?" Finch tilted his head slightly. "No one bears you any ill-will either?"

Cora wrung her hands. "No. No one."

Angie shifted in her seat. Something about the conversation bothered her, but she didn't know what it was. "Did the police find any clues about your husband's movements that day? A bit of clothing? Did anyone spot him somewhere, however briefly? Anything like that?"

"Richard disappeared into thin air." Cora bit her lower lip. "It's as if he was here one minute and then the next minute, he disappeared into the atmosphere like a puff of smoke."

"I'm clutching at anything I can think of," Jenna said. "Did your husband possibly get some bad news that made him run away? Had he recently been to the doctor? Maybe he heard some health news that he couldn't handle?"

"The police brought that up and paid a visit to Richard's doctor." Cora fiddled with her empty teacup. "Richard was as healthy as a horse."

"What about finances? Could bills or money troubles have upset him?" Courtney questioned.

"We didn't have any money issues. We have the usual bills, mortgage, car loan, some school loans for our boys. Nothing we couldn't manage."

"Did your husband have brothers or sisters?" Finch asked. "Are his parents alive?"

"Richard was an only child. He didn't know his father. His mother passed away when he was a young man."

Courtney noticed Cora's empty cup and poured more tea for her. "What about friends of your husband? None of them were contacted by him after he went missing? No one has an idea about what might have happened to him?"

Cora slowly shook her head.

"Forgive me for asking this." Mr. Finch's face was serious. "But how was your relationship with your husband, Mrs. Connors? Did you have disagreements? Was this a particularly stressful time for any reason? Were the two of you not getting along?"

Cora's cheeks flushed. "We'd been married for twenty-four years when Richard went missing. We got married when I was twenty and Richard was twenty-one. We had times when we had quite a few disagreements, but we stayed together. This wasn't one of those times."

"How did you meet your husband?" Angie

smiled at Cora.

"We met in college. We were practically inseparable." A little smile played over the woman's lips. "We got married right before my junior year and his senior year. We got an off-campus apartment."

"What did you both study?" Jenna asked.

"I studied to be a teacher. Richard studied business."

"You've had a career as a teacher then?" Finch questioned.

"I worked even when our boys were little. I teach math. I have over twenty years in."

"Are you planning to retire soon?" Angie wondered if the woman was having any financial problems since she no longer had her husband's income.

Cora shook her head. "I enjoy my work. It's also a distraction. I like getting out of the house and talking with my colleagues. Going to work kept me from losing my mind after Richard went missing."

Angie made eye contact with Cora. "I know that some of our questions are very personal, but if you want our help finding your husband, it's necessary for us to ask."

Cora gave the slightest nod.

Angie brought up the question of money again. "Now that you're husband is missing and you no longer have his income, are you struggling financially?"

"I'm okay. Of course, I miss the other income, but I'm able to handle our bills, so I'm doing okay."

Angie followed-up with another question. "Did your husband access any of your bank accounts after he went missing?"

"Nothing, no." Cora's lip trembled. She started to speak and then stopped. She took a swig of her tea and set the cup down on the saucer before sucking in a breath. "After Richard went missing, my friend suggested that I should hire a private investigator to look into my husband's disappearance. I don't know why I didn't do it, but I held off. Maybe I was still too shell-shocked by the whole thing. Two weeks ago, my friend showed me an old article about you people helping to solve a case."

Angie wanted to roll her eyes. *That danged article.* This wasn't the first time someone called on the Roselands and Mr. Finch to help them after reading that old news article.

"Richard's been missing for four months now." Cora's eyes were moist and she wiped at them with her hand.

"You feel that now is the time to bring in some outside help?" Jenna asked.

"No ... well, yes. It's not only that time has passed and it's been a long time without any new information and without any breaks or leads in the case." A tear rolled down the woman's cheek and she batted at it. "Something happened recently."

Everyone around the table sat straighter. Euclid and Circe perked up and stared at Cora waiting to hear what she had to say.

"One of Richard's credit cards." Cora sucked in a deep breath and pushed at her bangs. "There's been activity on one of Richard's credit cards."

Angie's heart beat sped up. "You told the police about it?"

Cora shook her head vigorously. "No."

Courtney's eyes widened in surprise. "Why not? It could be an important break in the case."

Cora's eyes narrowed. "It could also be a message."

The puzzled expressions of the four people around the table faced Cora.

"I don't want the police to scare him."

"Scare who?" Mr. Finch asked.

"Richard. What if he's trying to contact me? What if it's a message? What if using the credit card is his way of telling me he's alive?"

At that comment, everyone's mouths hung open.

CHAPTER 6

"Alive? You think Richard is alive and using his credit card?" Angie didn't know what to make of this.

"But it's been four months since he's been gone." Jenna spoke gently. "Weren't all of his credit cards cancelled when Richard disappeared?"

Cora's eyes looked brighter. "Richard kept one card especially for emergencies. I told the police to keep that card open in case he needed to get home."

"So you have your husband's wallet and that one card is missing from it?" Courtney asked. "He must have had it with him when he went missing." Courtney and the others thought this was important. If Richard had taken a credit card with him, he may have deliberately taken off.

Cora looked from one person to the next. "Yes. It was his emergency card."

"How can you be sure that he actually had the card on him when he disappeared?" Angie asked.

"I can't be completely sure, but I'm almost positive it was with him. Richard believed in being prepared."

"He always had it with him?" Jenna was skeptical. Maybe Richard planned to take off and made up the story about needing to have an emergency credit card.

"Always. He slipped it into his back pocket every morning without fail."

"When did he start doing this?" Jenna couldn't help but think how odd this was.

Cora thought. "About ten years ago? He'd read about a big flood down South. People had to flee with nothing. Richard was darned sure he would always have his card with him as a means to pay for food or a hotel."

Angie tilted her head. "Why would your husband use the card to let you know he was alive? Was it some prearranged signal that you two had worked out in case something happened?"

"No. We hadn't planned a signal or anything."

Angie pressed. "Then why wouldn't your husband get in touch with you using common means? Like a phone call."

"He might not think it was safe to do that." Cora frowned.

"What was the purchase that was made on his card?" Finch asked Cora, thinking that whatever was bought might be a clue to what was going on. "Was it only one purchase?"

"He bought some new clothes." Cora's voice sounded hopeful.

45

Courtney realized something. "Where were the purchases made? That would tell us where Richard, or whoever used the card, was when the purchase was made."

"The clothes were purchased in a mall in New Hampshire."

"In one store?" Angie suspected that someone found Richard's credit card and was using it.

"No, two stores."

"Were there any other purchases made?" Mr. Finch asked.

From the expression on her face, it was clear that Cora was thinking something over. "There was one other purchase. The credit card paid for one night in a motel room in New Hampshire." Cora leaned forward with a look in her eyes that Angie couldn't decipher. "Richard could be in the very next state."

Angie didn't know how to respond to Cora's statement. She watched the woman's face when she asked, "Why did you want to meet with Jack?"

"I want him to look into whether or not someone has stolen Richard's card." Cora closed her eyes for a moment. "I need to know if someone is using Richard's credit card or if it's Richard who's using it."

***

Ellie returned home from getting coffee with

Jack just as the family was moving into the family room at the back of the house so that they could talk freely and privately. The five people and two cats took seats on the sofas and chairs and settled in to talk over what they'd learned from Cora about the disappearance of her husband.

"Did Jack talk to you about Cora Connors and her troubles?" Courtney had snuggled into an easy chair with Euclid resting over her lap.

Ellie frowned. "He told me about her husband. I have to admit that I wasn't thrilled to hear the story. It worries me that the man is missing and no one has a clue as to what happened to him." A shudder ran over Ellie's shoulders. "I suppose nothing will happen, but I worry that whoever did something to the man might turn up here looking for Cora ... or us, if we agree to look into the case."

Jenna sat at the end of one of the sofas with Angie's legs stretched over her lap. "Did you tell Jack that we help the police sometimes?" Jenna wondered, as did the others, how Jack came to know that Police Chief Martin called on the sisters and Mr. Finch to help with difficult cases.

Ellie's eyebrows went up. "I never breathed a word. Jack asked me about it on the ski trip. I was going to tell you once we got home. Somehow, Jack figured it out all on his own. He didn't buy the tale we told about having counseling experience and that's the way we help the police. He saw that newspaper article about us helping the police solve that first case and he thought we must help Chief Martin with suspect profiles and the like. I told him he was right. I almost died when he brought it up fearing that he would ask about our 'special skills.'"

"He didn't, though?" Angie asked.

"No. There was no mention or hinting about any of us having special powers." Ellie looked sad. "I wish Jack knew about us. I don't like keeping it from him."

"I don't like keeping it from Josh either." Angie let out a sigh. "When do you tell someone? If you tell him early in the relationship, then he doesn't know you very well and he might run away and besides, I want to be sure I can trust the person before I start blabbing about the things we can do."

Ellie agreed. "Right. Then when *do* you bring it up? It never seems the right time. Then time goes on. I'm afraid Jack will be angry that we've been dating so long and I haven't told him." She groaned and rubbed her forehead. "What a mess." She looked over at Jenna. "You're lucky that Tom knows."

Jenna's fiancé was told several months ago about the sisters and Mr. Finch and their special abilities. Jenna nodded. "Yes, I'm glad that is done and out of the way and that Tom took it so well. It was a huge relief. I don't know what I would have done if I'd lost him over it."

Mr. Finch ran his hand over Circe's soft fur. "If

you lost Tom over it, Miss Jenna, then he wouldn't have been the man for you."

Ellie and Angie stared at Mr. Finch.

Angie tilted her head to the side. "You're right, Mr. Finch." She pushed up from her reclining position on the sofa and looked over to Ellie. "I think we should each talk with our men. Soon. I think it's time."

Ellie's eyes widened in fear, but then she shrugged her shoulders and gave a nod. "I dread it, but Mr. Finch is right. If it's something that is too difficult for Jack to accept, then Jack and I aren't the right match." Ellie brushed at her eyes and looked like she wanted to cry.

Courtney pushed Euclid's orange and white tail out of her eyes. "Don't worry, Sis. You and Jack are the right match. That leather business card holder that Nana left you had the initials ERF engraved on it. Ellie Roseland Ford. I knew the minute I saw that thing that you were going to marry Jack Ford."

Ellie's expression turned hopeful. "I hope you're right."

A round of teasing Ellie about her feelings for Jack ensued and the tall blonde pretended to be annoyed by the hoots and comments, but she actually enjoyed it and dished it right back to her sisters and Finch about their respective boyfriends and girlfriend. The topic ended with chuckles and giggles and then the group returned to the reason they'd moved into the family room.

Jenna stood up and walked to the desk by the windows where she started tapping on the keyboard of her laptop. "I'm looking for more stories on Richard Connors's disappearance." She stared at the screen. "There are tons of stories. A lot of articles are from early in the case." Scrolling through the listings of news stories, she said, "The articles get fewer as time goes by."

Angie took a seat next to her sister. "We have a lot of reading to do. Maybe we should split the stories between us and then we can talk about what we've learned."

"Good idea." Courtney yawned. "I'm getting sleepy. I didn't think we'd be back on a case just a few hours after returning from our ski trip." Smiling, she added, "But I like it."

"What on earth happened to that man?" Ellie asked. "How does someone disappear without a trace?"

"And motive seems to be missing." Courtney covered another yawn with her hand.

"I find that suspicious." Mr. Finch's forehead creased in thought. "Everything was wonderful in the Connors's home. No one had any problems. Everyone got along with everyone they'd ever encountered. Nothing was wrong with any member of the family ... so Mrs. Connors says."

"You think she's lying, Mr. Finch?" Angie asked.

"Perhaps, not lying. Perhaps, glossing over? Not seeing things clearly? Only seeing what she wants to see?" Finch rubbed the palm of his hand over the brass knob at the top of his cane. "As always, some digging is in order."

"And we are just the group to do it." Courtney winked at Finch. "But first, let's all watch a crime show together before we go to bed."

At that, Euclid trilled and Circe meowed as everyone settled comfortably in their seats trying to hold onto a few more hours of peace.

CHAPTER 7

Coming down the staircase, Angie could hear Mel Abel's voice booming away in the dining room where he and two other guests, along with Orla O'Brien, had gathered for breakfast. She successfully slipped unseen into the hallway from the foyer and made her way to the kitchen. Not knowing how late they would get in from their ski trip last night, Angie had arranged to take the morning off from the bake shop and her employee, Louisa, was handling the bakery duties.

Hurrying out of the kitchen carrying a tray of boiled eggs, toast, and jam, Ellie almost plowed into her sister. "Sorry." She made a face as she edged through the doorway. "How is it possible that that man's voice can be heard throughout the entire first floor of the Victorian? He's only been downstairs for thirty minutes and I already have a headache."

Angie smiled in agreement. Mr. Abel's voice was like a big bass drum shaking the walls and ceilings and she wondered if his voice had been an asset or a hindrance to him during his working years.

Courtney sat at the kitchen table in her pajamas eating a bowl of cereal and Jenna and Tom were perched on stools at the kitchen island drinking coffee and eating scrambled eggs. They greeted Angie when she came in.

"How are you up before me?" Angie stared at her twin sister. "Did I oversleep?"

Jenna grinned. "No, you didn't. I'm early this morning. Tom and I are heading to our house to get in a few hours of work before we tackle our real jobs."

Tom pulled on his earlobe. "And to get away from that man's voice."

Angie chuckled and put two slices of bread into the toaster as Mr. Finch came in through the back hall.

"Look who I found outside." Finch hung his coat on the rack and did the same with Chief Martin's.

"Morning." The chief nodded to the group in the kitchen.

Courtney looked up from her bowl of cereal. "Is there something wrong?" Her voice sounded almost hopeful.

"No, I just had coffee at the bake shop. Louisa said you were all in here so I came to say hello."

"How about a second cup of coffee?" Angie held the pot in the air.

"I wouldn't say no." The chief and Mr. Finch took the two other stools at the island.

"I was going to call you this morning." Angie

placed a mug of coffee in front of the chief and a cup of tea on the counter for Mr. Finch.

"What about? Is something wrong?" One of Chief Martin's eyebrows went up.

"No." Angie buttered her toast. "Well, yes."

The family told the chief about their B and B guest and the tale of her missing husband.

"I know that case. A strange one. The man was never found." The chief held his mug aloft. "It's like the man vaporized."

Ellie heard what the chief said as she came into the kitchen and made a face. "Ugh. What an awful word. Vaporized. It's like some science fiction story."

"There's been no trace of the man. Nothing." The chief took a swallow from his mug.

"Maybe someone put a spell on Mr. Connors and he went poof." Courtney spooned some cereal into her mouth without looking up.

Everyone in the room stared at her and sensing their gaze, she lifted her eyes. "Oh, come on. That isn't possible. Is it?"

"Ugh." Ellie shook her head and took a pot holder to remove a tin of blueberry muffins from the oven.

"I read some of the news articles online before I fell asleep last night." Angie carried her plate of toast to the kitchen table and sat down opposite Courtney. "The case is so strange that I couldn't stop reading. I stayed up way too late. Good thing

I have the morning off." She looked at Chief Martin. "Can you tell us anything about the Connors case?"

"That's a case that sticks in the minds of law enforcement agents. It's so puzzling. I know a detective in Mill City. The department worked like dogs to get a lead. Everything came up dry. They looked at the son, I don't recall his name, he'd just moved back home."

"What did they find out?" Jenna asked.

"The kid was mixed up with the wrong kind of friends. Drinking, probably some drugs, goofing off at school. The kid had to take a semester off in his freshman year because of his awful grades. Mrs. Connors claimed the son had recently come home to save money, but the officers down there wondered if the parents made him move home to keep an eye on him."

"Was the son a suspect?" Courtney questioned.

"He was initially. I think everyone was a suspect at first. There wasn't anything to pin on the kid. Of course, that doesn't mean he didn't have something to do with it."

"Did your friend think the son was guilty?" Tom took the last bite of his eggs and washed them down with a swallow of coffee.

"He said there was reason to be suspicious, but like I said, there wasn't any evidence linking the son to the disappearance."

"What about Mrs. Connors?" Angie eyed the

chief. "She was away for the weekend. She said her husband was missing when she arrived home. Did her weekend away with a friend check-out?"

The chief nodded. "She was at an inn on the New Hampshire coast with her friend. Trouble is, just because she checked in on Friday and checked out late on Sunday afternoon, doesn't mean she was there all weekend."

"True." Courtney used her spoon to poke the air for emphasis. "That very thing happened on an episode of a crime show we watch. Remember, Mr. Finch?"

"Indeed, I do." Finch got up to make some toast. "The friend of the criminal covered for him. Did the friend claim to be with Mrs. Connors the entire time?"

"I believe the friend told police that she and Mrs. Connors were apart for a few hours on Sunday morning. The officers didn't think that it was enough time for the woman to go home, kill her husband, dispose of the man, and return to the inn."

"What about friends, business associates, or other family members?" Tom wondered if there was some anger or resentment or whatever between Richard Connors and someone who might bear him a grudge.

Chief Martin shook his head. "Nothing stood out. Minor things here and there, but people's alibis were checked and validated."

"One of Richard Connors's credit cards was charged the other day." Angie frowned. "Mrs. Connors won't tell the police about it. She thinks Richard might be using the card to signal to her that he is alive."

The chief stared at Angie. "Why does she think he's doing that? Why not just pick up the phone and call his wife? Why the cloak and dagger act?"

Angie shook her head. "She didn't really have an answer for that question. She said he might not think it was safe."

Chief Martin's face screwed up. "Not safe from what?"

"We didn't get to that." Angie put her dishes in the dishwasher.

"What was purchased with the credit card?" the chief asked.

"Clothes," Jenna said. "Whoever is using that card bought clothes in two different stores."

"Where were the charges made?"

"The clothes were purchased in a New Hampshire mall. There was another charge." Courtney informed the chief. "A night in a motel room in New Hampshire."

"Huh," the chief grunted. "The most likely answer to this is that someone has Richard Connors's credit card."

"Yup." Courtney shrugged. "But it seems Mrs. Connors is inclined to think otherwise."

"Clutching at straws. Keeping hope alive," the

chief said. "We might do the same if we were in her shoes."

"She's asked for our help." Angie eyed the big man sitting at the island.

"It couldn't hurt." Chief Martin nodded and smiled. "I have it on very good authority that the five of you have an excellent track record with difficult cases."

"If we do try to help, could we run things by you?" Angie hoped to be able to bounce ideas and clues off of the chief.

"By all means." The chief slid off the stool. "I'd better get back to work." As he headed for the back hall to get his coat, he stopped and turned. "You know, I recall that the police brought someone in to consult on the case."

"Who?" Jenna asked.

"A psychic."

Everyone gaped at the chief.

"Really?" Courtney looked excited.

"Who was it?" Ellie's eyes were wide as saucers.

"I don't recall." The chief shrugged into his wool coat. "I could find out."

"Would you ask?" Angie thought it would be very helpful and slightly weird for them to speak to another person who had skills.

"Well," Tom noted, "the case wasn't solved so maybe that psychic wasn't very good."

"I'd still like to speak with the person." Angie poured herself another cup of tea. "The psychic might have come up with some ideas, but maybe there wasn't enough evidence to go forward."

Ellie leaned back against the counter with her arms crossed over her chest. "Is it possible Mr. Connors is still alive?"

"I'd vote probably not. It's been so long." Courtney rinsed her cereal bowl in the sink and then turned around and eyed Ellie. "Why? Do you feel something?"

Ellie blinked. "What? Me? No." She shook her head. "Nothing."

Courtney narrowed her eyes. "Yes, you do. You feel something."

Ellie turned away abruptly and headed out of the kitchen. "I have to check on the guests."

With her hand on her hip, Courtney looked at her sisters, Mr. Finch, and Chief Martin. "Yup. She feels something."

CHAPTER 8

"Cora Connors would like to speak to all of us."
Ellie came back into the kitchen right after Chief
Martin left to return to work. "Can we gather in the
sunroom to talk to her?"

"What have we decided?" Jenna asked. "Are we
going to look into her husband's disappearance?"

"I guess so." Angie wasn't thrilled about taking
on the case. There were things about it that made
her feel unsettled and wary.

The others agreed to give the case a look and if
things did not seem promising then they would give
up. They all traipsed into the sunroom to talk to
Cora who was sitting on the sofa by the windows
gazing out at the snow-covered yard. She turned
and gave the group a little smile. "Thank you for
meeting with me." She clasped her hands in her
lap. "I'll come right to the point. Would you be
willing to investigate my husband's
disappearance?"

Angie spoke for the group. "We've discussed it
and have agreed to have a look. It would just be an

initial gathering of information and checking out the leads that the police came up with. We can't promise anything. Law enforcement was unsuccessful and we probably won't have any better luck."

Jenna spoke kindly. "As long as you understand that, then we'll give it a try."

Cora beamed at them and thanked them all profusely. "I very much appreciate it."

Ellie sat straight in her seat and gave Cora a serious look. "You understand that we'll need total cooperation. Nothing will be discovered unless you and your sons are upfront with us. Holding things back or giving only partial answers to the questions we ask will not prove productive and will waste everyone's time."

Cora nodded.

"We'll do a preliminary investigation." Courtney was still wearing her pajamas. "If we think there is reason to continue, then we will of course, but we may have to end the inquiry if there isn't anything to go on."

"I understand."

Mr. Finch spoke next. "We have heard that a psychic was called in by the police. Can you share with us what that person came up with?"

One side of Cora's mouth turned down. "I thought it was nonsense to bring in a psychic."

Courtney rolled her eyes at Angie and gave her a half smile.

61

"The police wanted to do it anyway. They said the results were inconclusive."

"What does that mean?" Courtney asked. "Inconclusive? Did the psychic have some ideas or suggestions?"

"I don't know." Cora wrung her hands in her lap. "I didn't ask for details. I thought it was nonsense. Nothing came of it, so I didn't care to know any more."

"Do you recall the name of the psychic?" Jenna questioned.

Cora's eyebrows went up, surprised that the sisters and Mr. Finch would care about the psychic. "I don't know. I could find out for you."

Ellie nodded. "Yes, please find out."

Angie eyed Ellie, surprised that she was taking such an active role in the proceedings.

Ellie folded her hands in her lap. "I think the first step would be to visit your home in Mill City so we can look around and get a feel for the layout and where things allegedly occurred."

After Ellie spoke, each family member turned and stared at her.

"The sooner, the better," Ellie added. "And it would be helpful if your son, the one who was home the day your husband disappeared, is at the house when we arrive."

Discussion centered on when everyone could make the trip to Mill City and it was agreed that, since it would only take a little over an hour, they would drive down later in the day. Cora left the sunroom to phone her son.

"Who has taken over your body?" Courtney gave Ellie the eye.

The tall blonde blinked. "What do you mean?"

"In our other cases, you've been more reluctant to get involved." Angie pointed out the change in her sister's behavior.

Jenna smiled. "You're leading the charge this time."

"I just thought I should be more help." Ellie stood and headed out of the room. "I'm going to see if the guests need anything else on the breakfast buffet."

Courtney watched Ellie leave the sunroom and then turned to the others. "What's the real reason she's suddenly become the case manager?"

Everyone shrugged and shook their heads in amazement.

"Time will tell." Mr. Finch leaned on his cane and followed the others out of the room.

***

Ellie pulled her van behind Cora Connors sedan in the driveway of her home in Mill City. Courtney held Mr. Finch's arm as he maneuvered out of the backseat. The cats jumped out and sat on the brick driveway.

The house was a large two-story home with an

attached two- car garage and even though it was winter, the bushes and trees around the home were trimmed and well-cared for. The house looked freshly painted and nicely maintained and matched the other homes in the neighborhood in size and quality.

"This is where we live." Cora stood at the curb looking over the house she'd shared with her husband for so many years and marveled at the speed with which time had passed.

A barefoot young man wearing jeans and a baggy t-shirt opened the front door and waited for the guests to enter. Slender, bordering on skinny, with long legs and arms, his dark brown hair was mussed and he had some scraggy facial hair on his chin and cheeks like he was attempting to grow a beard. He ran his hand over his hair trying to push down the strands that were sticking up. Courtney got the impression he'd just woken from a nap.

The shoes and boots worn by Finch and the sisters made a scrunching noise as they moved over the sand and tiny bits of gravel that had been spread to give traction over some icy spots on the walkway from last night's freeze. Despite cold nights, the past week had seen unusually warm weather in Massachusetts and most of the snow had melted leaving just a dusting here and there over the lawns.

"This is our youngest son, Karl." Cora introduced the Roselands and Finch.

"You brought cats?" Karl watched the orange boy and the sweet black creature enter the foyer. "Why?"

"They travel with us," Ellie said.

"Why?" Karl persisted.

Courtney handed her coat to Karl and deadpanned, "They're good at solving mysteries."

Karl was about to chuckle, but stopped himself when it seemed that Courtney might be serious. One of his eyebrows arched in question.

Ellie gave her sister a look of disapproval and Courtney winked and shrugged in response.

"She's kidding," Jenna leaned in and whispered to the young man with a reassuring smile.

When everyone was inside and coats had been removed, Cora suggested that they all sit down in the large, comfortably furnished living room.

"I didn't realize there were so many of you," Karl remarked as he eyed Courtney in a leering way. She scowled at his attention.

"We're a family," Angie said. "We work as a team."

Karl didn't look impressed. "Have you had any luck solving cases?"

"We have." Jenna sat upright in the rocking chair.

"Cases as cold as this one?" Karl looked from person to person.

"Colder," Courtney told the young man. She didn't much care for Karl's mix of superior attitude and nonchalance and didn't think they'd be getting much that was useful from him.

Everyone sat in uncomfortable silence for a few moments unsure of how to start the inquiry so Angie spoke up. "Your mother has asked us to take a look at your father's case to see if we can find something that might have been overlooked."

Karl interrupted her with a chuckle. "I don't see how anything might have been overlooked. There must have been a million cops involved."

Cora looked down at her hands clearly wishing that her son would speak his mind in a less abrasive way.

"You'd be surprised what gets overlooked in investigations." Ellie sniffed.

"I just don't see how four girls, an older man, and two cats can do more than the cops did."

Euclid let out a piercing howl causing everyone to startle.

Giving the orange cat a look of reprimand, Angie pushed a lock of her hair behind her ear and cleared her throat. "There isn't very much going on with the investigation right now. Months have passed, nothing new has surfaced, and the police don't have the time to give the case that they did early on. Your mother wants to be sure that no stone is unturned. Things can be overlooked at the beginning of a case that, once time has passed, is later noticed as important."

"It's quite common for investigators to be

brought in a year or more after an incident has happened." Jenna, being careful not to be antagonistic in any way, turned to Karl. "We understand that you were the last one to see your father. Can you run through the day for us? It was a Sunday, wasn't it?"

Karl shifted around on the sofa and brushed his hand through his hair. "I was here. I slept late. Dad had gone to the coffee shop and brought back some donuts. I watched some TV while I ate breakfast. Dad was in his office doing some work for his business. I went up to shower. I was going out to meet some friends. When I came down to leave, Dad was mowing the lawn. I waved at him and he stopped the lawnmower, asked me what I was doing for the day. I walked to my car and Dad started mowing again. I left and met my friends."

Jenna asked, "What time was that?"

"A little after noon, maybe closer to 1pm."

"Where was your mom?" Mr. Finch knew where Cora was but wanted Karl to tell.

"She went to New Hampshire for the weekend."

"Alone?" Ellie asked.

"With her friend."

"Can you give us the friend's name?" Courtney had removed a pad of paper and a pen from her bag.

"Jill. Jill Jensen."

"Does she live in Mill City?" Circe had curled in Jenna's lap.

"Yeah. Jill and my mom work in the same school. They've been friends since high school. They went to the same college here in the city."

"What time did you come home after being with your friends?" Ellie questioned.

"Around 7pm." Karl rested back against the sofa.

"Who was here when you got home?" Finch took a turn asking a question.

"No one. The house was empty."

Finch sat upright with his cane between his knees and both hands on top of it. "Where was your father?"

"He wasn't here. I thought he must have gone for a run."

"And your mother?" Finch continued the questioning.

"She wasn't home from New Hampshire yet."

"Think back on the day." Finch looked Karl in the eyes. "I'd like you to remember little things. The weather, the look of the sky, how you felt ... bored, tired, energetic ... think about how your father seemed ... distracted, happy, rushed. Try to recall your interactions. Take a moment and immerse yourself in that day."

Slumped in his seat, Karl had his elbow on the arm of the sofa and his head against the palm of his hand. Angie wasn't surprised that the young man couldn't find a full-time job if this was how he presented himself to new people.

"Think about the little things of the day. Did your father get a phone call, an email that seemed to concern him? Perhaps a text came in that might have changed his mood? Any small thing that you might remember could shed light on what happened."

"It seemed like a normal day." Karl bit at the side of his fingernail.

Angie sighed at Karl's nonchalance. "When did your mother come home?"

"Around 8pm."

"No sign of your father though?"

Karl shook his head.

"And when your mother returned, what happened?"

Karl glanced at his mother. "She came home. I was watching TV. I'd heated up a frozen pizza. She asked where Dad was and I told her he hadn't been around since I got back."

"Then what happened?" Angie asked.

"I was in the den. I think Mom went to look in the garage to see if Dad's car was there."

"Was it?"

"Yeah."

"What did your mother do next?"

Karl looked over at his mom again. "I think she texted Dad. When he didn't answer, she called his phone." The young man cocked his head. "I think you called Mike then?" He turned back to Angie. "Mike's my dad's friend. Dad wasn't over there.

69

Mike said he hadn't heard from Dad all day."

"Then what?" Angie prodded.

"Mom called my brother. He didn't know anything. Mom waited until around 10pm and then she called the police."

"How did you feel then? Were you worried?" Ellie asked, wondering if Richard Connors had gone out on other occasions without informing his family where he was going.

"I figured Dad had gone for a long run or maybe ran into a buddy and maybe went for coffee or a drink. I really didn't give it any thought."

Courtney had been taking notes. She held her pen above the paper and asked, "If that was the case, why wouldn't your father answer his phone?"

"Who knows?" Karl gave a shrug. "Do you answer your phone every time it rings?"

"Yes." Courtney held Karl's eyes. "If it's someone in my family, I do. You don't?"

"Nope." A little grin played over the young man's mouth.

Angie looked over at Cora and moved to stand up. "I think it would be helpful if you could show us around the house and the grounds now."

As everyone stood and followed Cora and Karl from the room, Courtney leaned close to Angie and whispered, "And I think it would be helpful if Karl wasn't such a jerk."

CHAPTER 9

Cora led the group through the house pointing out the large kitchen at the back of the home, the laundry room where Richard had tossed his gardening clothes on the day he disappeared, and the downstairs closet where Richard's running shoes and deck shoes were lined up on the floor. Angie's heart gave a little squeeze of sadness when she saw the man's shoes still in their place after so many months. Cora led them to Richard's small office tucked off of the back hall. A few of them entered the room and the others stood in the hallway poking their heads inside.

"I assume the police went through everything? His laptop, emails, texts?" Ellie glanced around at the bookshelves, the file cabinets, and the neat stacks of papers on the desk.

Cora had to blink back a few tears. "The police went over everything. They went through the paperwork in the desk and the cabinets." She pointed at them. "Richard worked from home so this was where he kept everything."

"Did Richard only have one laptop?" Jenna moved around a little trying to pick up on anything.

"I never saw another one." Cora had her arms wrapped around herself. "Just the one, there on the desk."

"You've left his things the way he had them?" Mr. Finch ran his hand over the top of the chrome and glass desk.

"The police jumbled everything up and took the laptop for a while. But I tried to put things back in order. Richard didn't like things in disarray." Cora put her hand against her cheek. "I wanted everything neat for his return."

Angie took a quick look at Cora wondering why it was so important that things be *neat* and not in *disarray* for Richard.

The group was led to the upstairs bedrooms for a look around and when they returned to the first floor, everyone put on their coats and made their way out the back door to the yard. A few sprinkles of snow fluttered down from the gray sky and the air felt colder than when they had arrived with some biting gusts of wind kicking up every once in a while.

Karl gestured to where his father had been mowing the lawn at the front of the house when he'd come out to say goodbye to him before heading to meet his friends.

"What kind of a day was it?" Jenna moved around the yard.

"A typical beginning of September day." Karl scratched his cheek. "Sunny, almost hot, kind of humid. I remember because I didn't feel like running that day. I don't like humidity."

"Your father wasn't bothered by humidity?" Ellie asked. "He mowed the lawn even though it was hot and humid?"

"My husband was a disciplined man." Cora looked proud. "He did what needed to be done. He never let the elements stop him from working or exercising."

As they moved to the two-car garage, Angie wondered if that comment was a dig at Karl.

The garage had a shiny black sedan in the left side bay. Cora had parked her car in front of the house at the curb when they'd arrived from Sweet Cove. "This is Richard's car. The police went over it with a fine-tooth comb. They didn't find any evidence of foul play."

"Which would be expected." Karl had his hands shoved into the pockets of his jeans. "Dad only used the car in the morning that day."

The Roselands and Mr. Finch moved slowly around the garage with the cats padding softly about sniffing everywhere. As they walked by the car, Jenna and Finch discreetly placed their hands on the metal trying to pick up on any sensations.

A man's voice called out a hello and they all turned to see a tall, well-dressed young man with dark hair walking up the driveway. He gave Cora a hug and nodded to the group as his mother introduced her son, Roman. He smiled and shook hands with the Roselands and Mr. Finch. "Mom said she'd asked some private investigators to look into Dad's disappearance. I wasn't expecting five of you." Roman looked down at the cats. "Cats, too, huh?"

"We're really not private investigators." Angie corrected the man. "We're strictly volunteers and we never charge for our services. We have some experience so we help out when we're able."

Karl had a smirk on his face and Courtney glared at him.

"Well, it's nice of you to come by." Roman nodded. "I know mom appreciates any help. We all do."

"Roman works downtown. He's an insurance agent." Cora had her hand on her son's arm.

"I can only stay for a few minutes. I need to get back to the office, but I wanted to swing by to see if there was anything I could help with."

"Shall we go back inside for a few minutes, then?" Angie smiled. "We can go over some things before you need to get back to work."

"Glad to." Roman followed his mother to the door that led to the kitchen where everyone took seats at the large farm table that stood in front of huge glass windows that looked out over the yard. The snow flurries had stopped and the sun was trying to peek out from behind the whitish-gray clouds.

Angie asked Roman to give an account of his day on the date his father went missing and the young man told them how he'd gone kayaking on the nearby river with a young woman he was dating at the time. Afterwards they went for lunch and then he returned home to his apartment to do some paperwork. His mother called him in the evening asking if he knew where his father was.

"Had you spoken to you father that day?" Jenna asked.

"No. I spoke to him by phone the previous Friday about going to a baseball game the next week. My agency had some tickets that weren't going to be used and they offered them to me."

Courtney was making notes again. "That was the last time you talked to him?"

"It was." Roman let out the smallest of sighs.

"Did you get any sense that something was bothering your father?" Angie questioned.

"No. He was his usual self. There was no clue to indicate what would happen on Sunday."

Angie smiled. "Can you tell us what your father was like?"

Roman looked out of the window. "Dad was hard working. He liked to run, lifted some weights, nothing like a gym rat or anything, just to keep fit. Dad didn't go out much. He worked and he came home. He and mom were married for twenty-four years."

Something picked at Angie and she looked at Karl and Roman. "How would you both describe your relationship with your father?"

Roman glanced over at Karl and answered first. "We got along fine. Dad worked a ton. He wasn't one of those dads who was always playing sports with his kids or treating their kids like a best friend. I thought of Dad as sort of an old-fashioned kind of father, engaged in his work, supportive of the family, expected us kids to do well in school and become good members of the community."

Angie asked another question. "Did you go on vacations together?"

Roman replied again. "We'd take a hike together sometimes or go to the beach for a long weekend. Dad was careful with money. He thought kids should be out playing with other kids in the neighborhood, riding bikes, playing pick-up games, not having things organized for them."

"How about you, Karl?" Angie looked over at the youngest brother. "How would you describe your relationship with your father?"

"The same as Roman did." Karl gave a lazy shrug. "Nothing much to add."

Angie took a quick look at her sisters and Mr. Finch and everyone seemed satisfied that they'd done what they could for the day and that it was time to go home.

Cora told her sons that she was returning to Sweet Cove for a few days and that they should call her if they needed anything.

The family piled into the van and Cora followed behind in her own car as they made their way to the highway for the hour-long trip back to Sweet Cove.

From the front passenger seat, Courtney let out a groan. "Guess what? As we were leaving the Connors's house, someone asked me out."

Jenna smiled at her youngest sister. "Roman?"

"Guess again." Courtney scowled.

Mr. Finch chuckled. "I saw Mr. Karl staring at you more than once. Perhaps opposites attract, Miss Courtney?"

"Not in this case, they don't."

"I think you should go out with him." Ellie grinned. "He might reveal some important information to you."

Courtney flicked her eyes to Ellie. "I'll tell Karl *you're* attracted to his bad boy ways and would love to date him, and then *you* can interrogate him about his father. Shall I give him your number?" she teased.

"You know," Jenna smiled at Courtney, "I'm sure Rufus wouldn't mind if you went out with Karl as long as it was in the spirit of doing good."

"Maybe *he* wouldn't mind," Courtney said. "But *I* sure would."

Turning the conversation back to the case, Angie asked, "So what were everyone's impressions?"

"It sounds like Richard Connors was sort of uptight." Courtney offered her opinion. "You heard

Cora say that Richard liked things in order. That she wanted things to be neat for when he returned. I think that's kind of weird. Maybe Richard was obsessive-compulsive."

"That's a good idea." Angie nodded. "That goes along with his thing of only wearing deck shoes all the time."

"And he seemed to keep tight control of the money," Ellie said. "I also got the impression that the man really wasn't that close to his sons. From what they said, he maybe didn't spend much time with them."

Jenna and Mr. Finch looked at each other.

Jenna spoke first. "When I touched the desk and the car, I had the strange sensation that Richard wasn't as wonderful as his wife and son claimed. I felt something I can't really describe, but something was off." She looked at Mr. Finch for confirmation.

Euclid rested across Finch's lap and listened as the older man gave his opinion.

"I think Miss Jenna is on to something." Finch nodded solemnly. "I suspect that Mr. Richard may be a more complicated man that what we've heard so far."

Euclid let out a hiss and Mr. Finch gently stroked the large boy's orange fur. "I believe Euclid agrees with us. I also believe it would be prudent to start looking into the life of Richard Connors. We may find out some things about him that have not yet come to light." Finch narrowed his eyes. "In fact, I would bet on it."

CHAPTER 10

The Roselands, Mr. Finch, the two cats, and Cora entered the foyer of the Victorian to find Orla O'Brien and Mel Abel sitting at the dining room table playing cards with Courtney's boyfriend, Rufus, Jenna's fiancé, Tom, and Chief Martin. There were two bowls of popcorn on the table along with a bottle of wine and five glasses. When the entourage arrived in the foyer, the five card players looked up and greeted them.

Chief Martin had texted Angie to ask when the group would be returning home as he had some information to share with them. Since the sisters and Finch were running late, the chief was enlisted to play.

"I came to see if you wanted to go to dinner." Holding his cards in his hands, Rufus, a recent transplant to Sweet Cove from England, smiled at the pretty honey-blonde who walked to his seat and hugged him. "I called a bunch of times," he said. "You didn't answer your phone."

"I had it turned off," Courtney told Rufus.

"I told him you went out on business." Tom nodded and stood up to greet Jenna. "You were all gone longer than we thought so we decided to join in the card game."

Orla eyed Jenna. "Was it a fruitful visit?"

Euclid and Circe had jumped up to their usual perch on top of the dining room cabinet and stared down at Orla.

Jenna stood behind Tom's chair with her arms wrapped around his shoulders wondering what Orla knew about their journey to Mill City since no one told the guests where they were going when they left the house. "It was a good day."

Mel held his cards in one hand and used his other to push a handful of popcorn into his mouth. He wiped his fingers on a napkin as he chewed. "I've decided," he announced in his booming voice, "that the best part of traveling is meeting new people."

"I agree with you." Orla considered which of her cards to play. "It is one of the most enjoyable things about visiting new places."

"That young man of yours is a real card shark," Mel informed Courtney. "I'm only glad we aren't playing for money."

Rufus smiled, enjoying the praise, and took a card from the pile in the center of the table.

"Don't feed his ego, Mr. Abel." Courtney smiled. "His head will swell and he won't be able to fit through the doorway."

Mel threw back his head and let out a belly-laugh. "You're a lucky young man, Mr. Englishman. A woman who is attractive, smart, and funny."

Rufus looked up at Courtney and then at Mel. "How do you know she's smart?"

"I see it in her eyes." Mel tossed down one of his cards.

"Now whose head is swelling?" Rufus teased his girlfriend.

Seconds later, the card game ended with groans from all of the players except Rufus who cackled with delight.

"I can't believe he won again." Mel moaned and threw down his cards in defeat.

Chief Martin stood and made eye contact with Angie and she nodded and the two of them went down the hall to the kitchen.

Ellie announced to the guests, "I'll set the buffet table with the evening refreshments. It'll just be a few minutes." She hurried down the hall to the kitchen.

Mel collected the playing cards into a pile. "I'll go freshen up and be back to enjoy the refreshments. Back in a flash."

Ellie and Mr. Finch headed to the kitchen where Angie and the chief waited for them before they started the discussion of the case of the missing man.

The chief pulled a piece of paper out of his

pocket and placed it on the kitchen island. "That's the name and number of the psychic that the Mill City police called in to consult on Richard Connor's case."

Angie poured tea and coffee for Chief Martin and Mr. Finch and then she helped Ellie prepare the platters and baskets with cookies, blueberry crumble cake, date squares, and fruit salad.

"Did the police officers in Mill City tell you what the psychic had to say?" Finch took a sip of the hot tea.

"They told me some of the things." The chief added some cream to his coffee. "The psychic was kind of cryptic about the man. He said that it was difficult to get a handle on Connors, but claimed that he felt the man was alive and perhaps, had left of his own accord."

"Really?" Angie brought the men a small plate with a few sweets for them to nibble on. "Alive, huh?"

"The police had the same feeling about Connors. There was absolutely no evidence of foul play that they could find. They sort of threw up their hands thinking that the case had lots of characteristics of a man just taking off." Chief Martin shrugged. "You can't force someone to go home. You can't force someone to stay at home either."

"Why would the man leave home like that?" Finch pondered what the motivation might be.

The chief tossed out some ideas. "Mid-life

crisis? Boredom? Another woman? Maybe he had some vague feeling that he hadn't enjoyed life enough?"

Angie filled containers with coffee, decaf coffee, and a third one with hot water for tea and placed them on the rolling beverage cart. "I know his doctor said Connors was healthy, but what if the man had been to a specialist and received bad news about his health. That might have made him run off."

"But," Chief Martin said, "There would have been an insurance payment made to the specialist and the police would have found out who he had seen."

"Unless, Connors paid cash and bypassed insurance." One of Angie's eyebrows went up.

"My buddy in Mill City also told me something interesting."

All eyes turned to the chief.

"Apparently, the psychic just recently got in touch with the police and said he'd like to come in and talk to them again about Richard Connors."

"The psychic has some new information?" Angie looked hopeful.

"So it seems. I think you'll have to talk to the psychic *after* he meets with the police. Depending on the information, the police may ask him not to reveal his new ideas to anyone else."

"That's understandable." Ellie placed the bowl of fruit on the rolling cart.

"What do you think?" Angie asked her sister. "Do you have any feelings or intuition about the case?"

Ellie stood holding a large platter. "I've felt from the beginning that the man is alive." Frowning, she added, "But I don't think he wants to be found."

"So you don't think he's sending his wife a message by using his credit card?"

"I hate to say it, but I don't think he is. I bet Jack will tell Cora that the card information has been compromised and is being used by someone else." Ellie pushed her hair over her shoulder. "Poor Cora. It would be awful to discover that someone you love has run away from you."

"I wonder." Angie went to the cabinet to get a stack of small dessert plates. "Cora seems slightly insecure. Richard seemed to control the finances and what the family did and Cora gives me the impression that she just went along with whatever Richard wanted."

"Mr. Karl is quite defensive," Mr. Finch noted. "He doesn't seem to have gotten on well with his father. It would be interesting to look at the young man's background and perhaps, to sit and talk with him alone, without his mother present."

"Karl liked Courtney." Ellie smiled and pushed the food and beverage cart out of the kitchen. "Maybe he'd open up to her, if she interviewed him by herself."

Mr. Finch looked at Angie with a little grin. "It

might be a hard-sell to get Miss Courtney to try that."

Chief Martin picked up a cookie from the plate. "My friend in Mill City told me that Richard had worked at an appraisal agency, years ago before he started his own business. Some people who knew Richard are still working there and they didn't exactly sing the man's praises. It might be worth having a chat with them."

"That's a great idea." Angie took some flour and sugar from under the cabinet to make some pastry items for the next day's bake shop inventory. "I'd also like to talk to Cora's parents if they're around. I wonder what they thought of Richard. It might help to get some impressions from family members and the couple's friends."

"There is much to do." Finch nodded.

"Tomorrow afternoon Jenna, Courtney, and I are taking a ride to the New Hampshire motel where Richard's credit card was used. We're going to show some pictures of him to the desk clerk." Angie told Mr. Finch, "I'm also going to make an appointment with the psychic. Maybe you can arrange your schedule at the candy store so that you can come along to interview the psychic with me?"

"I'd be glad to join you, Miss Angie. Just let me know when we're going."

Angie mixed ingredients into the stainless steel bowl and prepared a tart pan and some muffin tins while Finch and Chief Martin talked about the weather, world news, and town happenings.

As soon as Angie placed the muffin tins into the oven and set the timer, she leaned against the counter. "I can't stop thinking about the psychic. It's not that late. Do you think it would be okay to call now and set up a meeting with him?"

The chief looked up at the wall clock to check the time. "Sure, call. If the man doesn't want to speak right now, the call can go to his voice messages."

Angie hurried to the counter to pick up her phone and leaning down to see the psychic's number on the piece of paper that the chief had brought along, she pressed the numbers on the screen of her phone to place the call. Just as Angie thought the voice mail was about to come on, someone picked up on the other end so she introduced herself and told the person who she wanted to speak with and why. Mr. Finch and the chief watched Angie's expression change from concern to shock.

"I'm very sorry." Angie ended the call and turned to the two men sitting at the kitchen island. When she reported what the person on the phone had just told her, the looks on Finch's and the chief's faces shifted to match Angie's expression.

"The psychic is dead."

CHAPTER 11

Jenna sat in the driver's seat of her old car with Courtney beside her and Angie sitting alone in the back.

"That's awful about the psychic." Jenna pulled the car into the middle lane of the highway. "I wonder why he called the police recently and wanted to talk with them about Richard's case."

"He must have found out something about Richard or maybe he had a new idea." Courtney removed her leather gloves and placed them on the center console. "We'll never know now."

Angie sighed and gave her head a slight shake trying not to fall asleep in the car. She'd been awake all night, her brain buzzing over the psychic's death and what he might have wanted to talk over with the Mill City police detectives. "Ellie wonders if the psychic didn't die of natural causes."

"What?" Jenna looked into the rearview mirror to see her sister's face. "She said that?"

Angie nodded. "Ellie finds it suspicious that the man died shortly after arranging a meeting with the police. If foul play isn't involved, then Ellie thinks that whatever was on the psychic's mind worried him to death."

"I agree with her." Courtney glanced back at Angie. "Mr. Finch and I are suspicious as well. This sort of thing often happens in the crime shows we watch."

"It's kind of far-fetched. How would someone know that the psychic contacted the police?" Angie was skeptical that someone had killed the man to keep him quiet.

"Easy." Courtney pointed at the upcoming exit. "Maybe someone in the police department can't be trusted. Maybe that person told someone that the psychic had called. Maybe that person doesn't want any new information coming to light about Richard. Maybe the psychic confided his new information to someone who had something to do with Richard's disappearance."

"I can't believe that's what happened." Angie shook her head. "He most certainly died of natural causes."

"Did the psychic live in Mill City?" Jenna eased the car onto the exit ramp.

"The chief said he did." Angie watched the scenery pass by. "Are psychics more prevalent than we think? Are psychics walking around in *every* town and city? Do we pass them on the street all the time?"

"And I thought we were special." Courtney

harrumphed. "The psychic lived in the same city as the missing man. Maybe they have the same friends or acquaintances so that would make it easy to spill information to the wrong person."

Jenna's eyes widened. "Richard Connors might have found out that the psychic had important information and was about to talk to police. He might have returned to Mill City and killed him."

"First we need to hear from Chief Martin if the police in Mill City suspect foul play." Angie's first impulse was to dismiss the notion that the psychic met his death at the hands of someone involved with Richard Connors. "If the psychic died under odd circumstances, then maybe we can visit his wife and ask her what she knows."

"A visit to the wife might be helpful even if the psychic died of natural causes," Jenna pointed out. "His wife might know something. We might be able to find out why the man wanted to speak to the police again."

"Good thinking." Angie looked out the window as they passed a strip mall and some fast food restaurants. The branches of the few trees standing here and there were bare and some small grimy snow piles could be seen at the corners of parking lots. The sky was slate gray and the light levels were low from the heavy cloud cover.

Courtney spotted a rundown, one level motel coming up on the right side. "There's the motel up ahead." A metal sign was screwed to the front of the place and some of the lit-up letters had burned out so that the words "Beacon Motel" seemed to spell "Bacon Mol."

Jenna pulled into the lot and parked the car in a spot near the reception door. The sisters sat looking around for a few moments before getting out. The place had seen better days. There were about twenty rooms in the L-shaped motel with the doors to the rooms opening directly out to the parking lot. Paint was peeling, a few shutters hung askew, and the windows looked grimy.

"Not a five-star hotel," Courtney noted.

"I'm not sure it would earn one-star." Jenna scowled at the condition of the place. "Let's get this over with and get out of here."

When they opened the front door a bell jangled, and the chubby man behind the desk startled awake. The man's round cheeks resembled those of a squirrel whose mouth was filled with nuts. Rubbing his eyes, he pushed himself up and mumbled hello. His eyebrows shot up when he saw the three young women before him. "Are you checking in?" The desk clerk's tone was one of disbelief.

Angie smiled and approached the desk where she placed the large manila envelope containing the pictures and snapshots of Richard Connors. "We wondered if we could show you some photos of someone. The man has been missing for months and his family is very concerned about him. It seems that his credit card was used to pay for a room here not long ago." She told the man the date that the credit card was charged for the motel room. "Were you working that night by any chance?"

The desk clerk blubbered something incomprehensible as he checked the large calendar that covered his desk. "That was a Thursday. I always work on Thursdays."

"Great." Courtney gave the man a warm smile. "It would be a big help if you could look at the pictures we brought. Maybe you might recognize the man."

The clerk's thinning red hair was combed-over and plastered to his head. "I could take a look. Can't make any promises though. We get a lot of folks in who stay only one night. There's a lot of turnover here. I don't remember most people unless there's something that stands out about them."

Angie opened the envelope and shook it slightly to empty the photos onto the countertop. She moved them around so that they faced the desk clerk.

The man put on reading glasses and screwed up his face as he looked from one photo to the next, each one showing a smiling, athletic, nicely-dressed Richard Connors. Glancing up, the clerk looked over the rims of his glasses. "This guy doesn't look like most of our clientele, you know. We get guys like this in here, but it's the woman he's with who does the check-in and registration. The guy sits in the car."

Jenna nodded. "This man might not look quite the same way that he used to. He might have dyed his hair and let it grow. He's probably dressing down, jeans, a work shirt, things like that."

"I'd like to help you gals, but I don't know. I don't recognize this dude."

The sisters knew it was a long shot for Richard Connors to be recognized.

"The credit card he used that night has the name Richard Connors on it." Angie looked hopefully at the clerk. "Do you recall that name?"

"That's a pretty simple name. Nothing about it stands out."

"Did you have a lot of people checking in that night?" Jenna asked.

"One night is the same as the others." The clerk raised a shoulder in a shrug. "I don't pay much attention. I take the cash or run the credit card and give them the key, that's it. Unless someone causes commotion, then I sit quietly in here."

The sisters were about to thank the man for his help when something caught Courtney's eye at the top of the wall near the ceiling behind the desk. Her heart skipped a beat. "Is that a security camera?"

The desk clerk glanced over his shoulder to the ceiling. "Yeah."

Angie's heart started to race. "Does it work or is

it a fake?"

The desk clerk looked slightly offended by Angie's suggestion that the device might not be the real thing. "Of course it works."

"How many days of film does it record?" Courtney had to hold herself back from leaping over the counter.

"Two weeks."

"Can you look through the film? Can you show it to us?" Angie was so excited that she almost crushed the photo she was holding in her hand.

"We're not supposed to do that." The clerk had a grave expression on his face.

"What if we made it worth the trouble?" Jenna took her wallet out of her bag. "We know it would be a pain. We'd be more than happy to pay you for your time."

The guy's eyes widened when he saw Jenna's wallet. "I'm only supposed to show the film to the cops, you know. Not regular people."

"We're consultants with the Sweet Cove, Massachusetts Police Department," Courtney announced in an official sounding voice. "You can call the number there and ask for Chief Martin if you'd like to verify our affiliation."

The clerk blinked several times and then pushed himself out of his seat. "I don't need to call. I didn't realize you were with the police. Hold on and I'll get the tape from the camera." The man scurried away to the back room to get a step ladder.

The sisters high-fived each other.

"This could be a break." Courtney rubbed her hands together.

"Good eyes, Sis." Jenna patted her youngest sister's back. "I never would have noticed the camera."

The clerk came back carrying the step stool which he placed against the wall and shakily started up the few steps with one hand on Courtney's shoulder to steady himself. After a couple of minutes of stretching for the device and puffing like he'd just run a marathon, the clerk stepped down from the stool with the camera in his hand, a triumphant look on his face. The sisters applauded the man's mighty effort.

The desk clerk opened the camera. "See, it's not really film. It's a DVD thingy." He sat down in his chair and rolled it over to the desk where he inserted the object into the disc drive on the computer. After some clicking with his mouse, a grainy image showed on the screen. "Here we go. It takes a while. It's an old computer."

The three young women gathered around behind the man to watch the black and white images move across the screen. Most of the video showed the desk clerk asleep in his chair.

"Can we fast forward to the right date?" Jenna asked.

"Nuh-uh. If we do that, the screen goes dark." The screen already looked pretty dark to the

Roselands. It was more like watching shadows move around than actual humans.

Angie leaned closer. Sometimes the screen grew brighter and some facial features of a customer at the registration counter were visible. An hour of torture passed with all four of them watching the video. Courtney had been to the vending machine several times to buy bags of potato chips and corn chips which she shared with her sisters and the desk clerk. Crumbs and empty chip bags were strewn over the reception desk when, at last, the date of Richard Connors's supposed visit to the motel appeared on the screen.

Three men and two women registered separately that night. One of them had the body type of Connors so the clerk stopped the progression of the video so the sisters could stare at the man's face which was dark and fuzzy.

"I don't know." Courtney sighed and stood straight rubbing her eyes. "It's too grainy to make anything out."

"Maybe the police could take the disc and do something to it to make it clearer." Angie's back was stiff and sore from hunching forward to see the images.

"Can't give it to you." The clerk shook his head sadly. "I'd need a detective to ask for it."

"Can you keep it safe for us?" Jenna looked at the man. "Could you put it somewhere safe until the police can come up and get it?"

"I'll put it in the safe." The man extracted the DVD from the computer and slid it into an envelope.

The girls thanked the man warmly and headed for the door when the clerk spoke up. "Can I answer any more questions?"

"You've been a big help." Angie smiled at him and thanked the clerk again. "But I guess that's all we need for now."

The desk clerk's pudgy cheeks tinged pink and his face seemed to fall in disappointment. "Come back anytime. I liked helping you."

When they stepped outside, a biting cold wind blasted across the open parking lot as the young women climbed into Jenna's car and slammed the doors.

Sitting in the front passenger seat, Courtney looked through the windshield at the entrance to the motel's reception desk. "You know, when we first got here I didn't think that guy was going to be any help. I was wrong. He wasn't at all what he seemed."

He wasn't at all what he seemed. Angie wondered if that statement might also apply to Richard Connors.

CHAPTER 12

Looking out at the backyard of the Victorian, Cora Connors sat alone in the soft, white easy chair by the sunroom window with a cup of tea in her hand. She turned her head when Angie came into the room and looked hopefully at the young woman who sat down across from her.

"The desk clerk didn't recognize the pictures of your husband or his name."

The hope drained out of Cora's face.

"There was a security camera though. We looked through the video and someone who matched your husband's description was seen on the film."

When Cora's eyes grew wide, Angie quickly described the condition of the images on the tape to keep Cora from becoming unreasonably optimistic. "We couldn't make out the facial features of the person. Really, all we could tell about the person was that it was a male about your husband's height. The body shape and size were similar, but many people match that description. It's a possibility, but an extreme long shot."

Cora gave a nod and Angie could see different emotions flash over the woman's face as she considered the possibility that her husband might have been in the New Hampshire motel. Angie leaned forward and spoke softly. "Cora. You know this probably isn't Richard."

"Oh, I know that." Cora tilted her head slightly. "But it could be."

Angie sat back suppressing a sigh. "We've told Chief Martin about the tape. He'll be in touch with the Mill City police and they'll probably pick up the video and try to enhance it in order to get a clearer image of the person."

Cora held her teacup and its saucer and when she spoke, she tried to keep her voice steady. "How long will that take?"

Angie shook her head. "I have no idea. I don't think it's a quick process. You can speak to Chief Martin about it." Wanting to hear more about Richard, Angie asked a question. "Can you tell me more about your husband? He worked out of your house?"

"He did." Thinking of her husband caused some tears to show at the corners of Cora's eyes. "He had the office at home. Appraisers are often on the road, so Richard didn't need a separate place to meet clients or anything like that. He arranged his meetings over the phone or the internet. The home office was all he needed."

Angie remembered that Chief Martin told her that Mr. Connors had worked for an appraisal firm when he first started out. "Before going out on his own, Richard worked for a company?"

Cora nodded. "When he first started, he worked at a company for about five years to get training and experience. The idea was always to eventually do his own thing."

Angie asked the name of the company and where it was located and Cora provided the information.

"How did Richard like working there?"

"He didn't." Cora lifted her cup and sipped. "Richard preferred working on his own."

"Did he not like his coworkers?"

"They were fine."

"What about the boss? Did they not get along?"

"The boss was fine." The woman glanced out the window to the bare trees and the frosted back lawn."

"What didn't he like then?" Angie probed for more information.

Cora turned back to Angie. "Richard was his own person. He didn't like being told what to do. He didn't like working with a group of other people. He didn't like to be around a lot of people. Richard had strong opinions about things and how things should be done."

"Did he share his opinions at work?"

"Sure he did."

"Did his opinions cause trouble?"

Taking in a breath, Cora's face seemed to harden. "Richard could be ... oh, I don't know ... to others, he could seem pushy, a little impatient, aloof, but it was just his eagerness to get things accomplished and have them done right."

"So there was some friction in the workplace?" Angie used an even tone so that Cora wouldn't think that she was judging Richard.

"Some. Occasionally." Cora looked down at her cup.

"How about at home?"

Cora's head snapped up. "What do you mean?"

"Was there sometimes friction at home? Was Richard sometimes pushy or impatient at home?"

A short, little chuckle that Angie thought seemed forced sounded in Cora's throat. "No one's perfect. We're all impatient at times. We all get cranky or pushy or tired."

Angie smiled in agreement. "You mentioned when we were at your house that your husband liked things in order. Was he a neat freak?"

Cora waved her hand in the air. "Richard was organized. He liked everything in its place. He wasn't obsessive or anything, if that's what you mean."

Sensing that Cora might be feeling slightly defensive about her husband, Angie changed the topic. "How did you meet? Were you in some classes together?"

Cora's face softened as she looked across the

room thinking back on her college days. "No. I went to the library every evening, always sat in the same spot. Richard was often there, too. I'd catch him staring at me and when we'd make eye contact, he'd look straight down at his book. It went on for weeks. Finally, I got up from my chair one night and walked across the room. He looked up from his books and seemed shocked that I was standing in front of him. I smiled and introduced myself and then I went right back to my study table." Cora laughed recalling the incident. "Richard didn't know what to do, so he went back to studying."

Angie smiled at Cora, but was thinking about how her assertive behavior as a young college student didn't quite jive with the reserved, almost meek at times, middle-aged woman she seemed to have become. "How did the two of you end up dating?"

"I was at a concert on campus. I was part of the group that organized activities for students. We'd been able to snag a great band to play at school. I was at the front door taking tickets and Richard was standing outside. I caught him watching me so I waved at him." A look of pleasure passed over Cora's face. "He finally came over to me. He asked if I'd like to get a drink after the show."

"So you went?" Angie nodded.

"I had plans with some friends that night. We were going to the college pub after the concert. I invited Richard, but like I said before, he didn't like being with lots of other people so he didn't want to go. We arranged to meet the next night." Cora looked at Angie. "And the rest is history. We were together almost all of the time after that."

Angie couldn't put her finger on why, but something about what Cora was saying pinged in her head. "You told us that you'd married pretty quickly. Was it difficult to be married at such a young age?"

Cora's smile faded a little. "It wasn't hard, though marriage is an adjustment at any age. Richard was a quiet person who liked staying at home, studying, having a quiet evening while I had always been busy with college clubs and going out and seeing friends. Opposites attract, I guess."

"I guess." Angie nodded. "Did you grow up in Massachusetts?"

The smile returned to Cora's face. "Born and bred. I've lived in this state all of my life. I grew up right in Mill City. I didn't get far did I?" she kidded.

"How about Richard? Did he grow up in Massachusetts?"

Cora placed her empty teacup and saucer on the side table. "Richard had a difficult young life. He was born in South Carolina, but he and his mother moved around all the time. I think Richard lived in every New England state at least twice. There was never any money, they were always moving, he was always changing schools. The father wasn't in the picture, Richard doesn't even know who his father is. His mother was an alcoholic and she was abusive to Richard. He ended up in foster care. The poor man never wanted to talk about it. It was a very traumatic time that he tried very hard to forget and put out of his mind."

Angie thought that this bit of news made a lot of sense in suggesting why Richard liked things to be in order and why he might not have enjoyed socializing with lots of people. He may have had insecurities which had developed from his unstable and insecure background that caused him to shy away from people. The trouble with his coworkers may also have stemmed from his childhood insecurities. "Did Richard ever reunite with his mother?"

Cora shook her head sadly. "He didn't. She wanted nothing to do with him. The woman ended up in prison for a while and later died of a drug overdose. It took a long time for Richard to reveal these things to me. Honestly, it was a miracle that he told me anything at all. It was just too painful for him to talk about." Looking at Angie, she lowered her voice. "Our boys don't know these things. They just know that their dad's parents died very young."

"I'll keep it in confidence and only share the information with my family and Chief Martin," Angie reassured Cora. "Have you heard from Jack Ford? Has he found out anything about the possible theft of your husband's credit card?"

Cora's shoulders sagged. "I haven't heard anything yet."

Two things bounced around in Angie's mind ... she was pretty sure that Richard wasn't the one who used his credit card at the New Hampshire motel, and the second thing was a vague, dark, uneasy sensation that grew every time she learned something new about Richard Connors.

CHAPTER 13

Jenna and her three sisters worked in the dining room of Jenna's old house painting the walls a soft blue-gray while Euclid and Circe prowled through the rooms of the spacious home. The renovations had been going on for months as Jenna's fiancé, Tom, worked on the place in between his business's construction and renovation projects and Jenna spent much of her free time from her jewelry business pulling old wallpaper down, repairing walls and trim, and painting the rooms. Tom kidded her that she'd learned so much and was so skillful that he was going to hire her for his construction company.

The sisters had the radio playing and when a favorite tune came on, the four of them began to bellow along with the singer at the top of their lungs. Euclid and Circe tore into the room from upstairs afraid that the wailing sounds from the dining room meant that the girls were hurt or in trouble.

When they saw the alarmed looks of worry on

the cats' faces, Jenna, Courtney, Angie, and Ellie burst out laughing.

"We're okay," Courtney assured the animals from high on the step ladder. "It's just our awful singing."

"Thanks for checking on us." Angie chuckled and bent to scratch the cats' cheeks being careful that the paint on the brush in her other hand didn't drip onto the felines' fur.

Assured that everything was fine, the big orange boy and the sweet black girl sauntered away to continue their prowling through the house.

Ellie carefully painted up to the edge of the wood trim boards. "It's nice to know they're always looking out for us." The two cats seemed to sense whenever any of the Roseland sisters were in trouble and they howled and carried on to let the others know when something was amiss.

Jenna poured some paint from the can into a smaller container. "I agree. Those two have some kind of sixth sense when it comes to us." Moving the drop cloth over to cover the floor near the section of wall she was working on, Jenna stood straight with a serious expression on her face. "Speaking of a sixth sense."

The others immediately stopped what they were doing and turned to stare at their sister.

"What is it?" Angie took a step closer.

"This house has been empty for ages." A woman named Katrina Stenmark had owned Jenna's house a long time ago. Katrina had inherited the home, which was two doors down from the Victorian, from her grandparents and she'd lived there with her husband and son for many years. When she died, Katrina had no living relatives so the ownership of the place was in question and it took years and years for the town of Sweet Cove to claim the house, which by then had fallen into terrible disrepair. In a surprising twist, the Roseland sisters discovered that their Nana had been friends with Katrina.

The sisters waited for Jenna to say more.

Flicking her eyes to Ellie, Jenna continued in a soft voice. "Katrina had *that necklace* in her possession." The necklace that Jenna referred to was, at that moment, locked inside a safe in the Victorian's office. The necklace had some special powers and just before she'd died, Katrina had passed the pendant for safekeeping to the Roselands' Nana.

At the mention of the necklace, Ellie's face blanched. "What about it?" The girls had been told that someone, sometime, would come to collect the pendant from them and Ellie couldn't wait to have the piece of jewelry gone, especially because protecting the thing had almost cost them their lives when the Victorian's carriage house burned in a fire with the girls locked inside. The girls discovered that Ellie was the one who was supposed to keep the necklace safe until the unknown person came to fetch it.

Jenna stirred the paint in her container. "It doesn't have anything to do with the necklace ... at least, I don't think it does."

Courtney wanted her sister to get to the point. "What are you talking about?"

"I've been thinking about the previous owner lately. I've been wondering about Katrina Stenmark and what her life was like." Jenna sighed and looked to each of her sisters. "Sometimes when I'm working here alone ... I have the feeling that I'm *not* alone."

Courtney's, Ellie's and Angie's eyes widened.

Courtney's voice bubbled with excitement. "You think there's a spirit here?" Glancing around with a smile, she added, "Cool."

Angie scrutinized her twin sister's face. "Does it worry you?"

"Not really." Jenna dipped her brush into the paint. "I just wonder why someone remains here in the house."

"You think it's Katrina Stenmark?" Ellie looked nervously over her shoulders.

"I don't know who it is." Jenna painted close to the trim board. "I haven't seen anyone. I just *feel* someone. Sometimes."

"Have you told Tom?" Angie questioned.

"Not yet. I wanted to tell you first because I'm not sure if I'm imagining it. I wanted to know if you ever sense anything when you're in here." Jenna looked from sister to sister.

"Whenever I'm here, I'm working so I don't pay attention." Courtney cocked her head and smiled. "But I will now."

"Is it a faint feeling?" Angie glanced out to the center foyer.

"When I'm alone, I sense it more strongly. If other people are here, I often don't feel anything at all." Jenna knelt to paint above the baseboard. "I haven't sensed anyone around today."

"I need to focus on it." Angie nodded. "Maybe the spirit only feels comfortable when it's just you here in the house."

Ellie made a face.

A sudden crash from above caused the four young women to jump and stare up at the ceiling.

"It must be the cats." Jenna placed her paint brush on the top of the paint can. "They must have knocked something over." She headed for the staircase with her sisters following behind.

"Don't leave me down here alone." Ellie hurried after the others and as she turned for the stairs, something in the living room caught her eye. "The cats are here curled up on that old beat-up sofa in the living room." The two felines had lifted their heads to see what was causing the commotion in the foyer. "They look like they've been sleeping." A worried expression passed over Ellie's face. "If the cats are here, then they didn't knock anything over upstairs."

Jenna, Angie, and Courtney halted their climb

up the staircase and looked down at Ellie who stood in the foyer with one foot on the step. Taking a glance up to the second floor landing, Jenna raised an eyebrow. "If the cats are downstairs, then what caused the noise up here?" Gripping the wooden banister, she slowly advanced with her sisters right behind her. "The sound came from the room over the dining room."

Four heads peeked into the space and, seeing nothing, they entered a room that had been previously used as a library. Wooden shelves filled with volumes of dusty books covered two of the walls, a fireplace stood to the right, and a large window looked out over the front yard towards Beach Street. Jenna and Tom had not yet removed all of the pieces of furniture that had remained in the house since they planned to keep some of the things and hadn't had time to decide what to hold on to and what to remove.

"This is really a beautiful room." Angie moved around the space. "It would make a great place to read or work on your jewelry designs. You and Tom could share it as an office."

An antique sofa stood in the middle of the floor. Carved walnut wood trim ran over the curved back of the piece, but the upholstery was ripped and worn. Jenna hoped to learn how to reupholster furniture so that she could restore the old couch.

"Tom loves this room." Jenna looked about the large space trying to find the source of the noise that they had heard from downstairs. "He's talked about sitting in here reading on a winter evening with a fire burning in the fireplace."

Courtney loved books and walked to the shelves where she ran her hand over some leather-bound volumes, bending to read the titles on the spines. "I didn't notice all of these old books when I was up here before. I bet there are some valuable first editions on these shelves. Katrina Stenmark must have been a collector."

"What made the noise?" Ellie stood at the threshold of the room. "Nothing seems out of place."

Euclid and Circe brushed past Ellie's leg and padded into the room where they inspected the four corners, looked up at the shelves, jumped on an old roll-top desk, and sniffed around the chairs and side tables.

Wondering if a breeze had come in through the window, Angie checked to be sure it was fully closed and locked. "The window's shut and the glass is intact so it wasn't the wind blowing through."

The cats sat side by side under one of the maple tables watching the sisters inspect the room. Euclid tired of supervising the young women so he let out a low growl which caused the four girls to stop and turn.

Courtney walked across the room, knelt on the floor, and patted the felines. "What's up, you two?" Peering under the table, she reached her hand to grasp something and stood up. "A framed picture was on the floor. The glass is cracked. Maybe it fell off the side table."

Everyone gathered around to look at the six-by-eight inch photograph that showed an older woman, flanked by two smiling men, sitting on the same antique sofa that still stood in the center of the room. Jenna turned it over and slid the picture out of holder being careful that the cracked glass didn't fall from the frame. On the back of the photo, the words *Katrina, Walter,* and *Ben* were written in careful script.

"It's Katrina Stenmark." Jenna smiled. "This must be her husband and son."

"The picture must have fallen off of the side table," Angie noted. "That must have been what we heard."

The sisters paused for a moment and then stared at each other when realization dawned on them.

"Oh." Ellie nervously pushed a strand of her long hair over her ear. "It was Katrina Stenmark."

"So." A look of delight showed on Courtney's face as she smiled at Jenna. "I guess your spirit decided to get your attention and stop playing hide and seek with you."

Jenna studied the photo in her hands. "I guess I *wasn't* just imagining her being in the house after all."

Courtney chuckled and headed out of the room. "You better tell Tom that once you move in here, there will be three of you living in this house."

CHAPTER 14

The late afternoon sun filtered through the windows as Jenna, Angie, and Mr. Finch sat in the living room of Cora Connors's best friend, Jill Jensen's house. Carrying a few extra pounds, the brown-eyed woman was in her mid-forties and exuded a warm manner. Her dark blonde hair was cut stylishly in soft layers around her face. Jill had made tea and coffee for the guests and the group had settled into conversation about the friendship between Cora and Jill and last September's disappearance of Richard Connors.

"Cora and I met in high school and became fast friends. We hung out together all the time. We had other girls in our group, but they came and went." Jill laughed. "Cora and I stuck together like glue." The woman told tales of her and Cora's adventures, their college years, getting jobs teaching at the same school, and their families.

"Cora and Richard married young," Angie observed.

Jill rolled her eyes. "I was against that, as you

can imagine. I didn't think she knew him long enough and I thought they should wait until after graduation to get married. My negativity about the marriage was partially due to knowing that Cora marrying Richard would cut into our friend-time and I wasn't ready to share my buddy with some man." Jill smiled and shrugged a shoulder. "I also wasn't crazy about Richard. I didn't think they were a good match."

Mr. Finch asked, "You didn't care for the young man?"

Jill waved her hand around. "Richard was too quiet. I didn't think he was enough fun. He was too serious and reserved. I thought he was hard to know."

Jenna placed her coffee mug on the table. "Did Cora consider your concerns and worries about Richard?"

"Cora was in love." Jill sighed. "Richard was her first serious boyfriend. I think she got sucked in by the attention Richard gave her." Jill leaned forward. "I thought it was smothering, if you want to know the truth. I had the feeling that Richard would try to push me out Cora's life."

"Did he do that?" Angie asked.

"At first, I felt like he did, but that could have just been jealousy on my part and not being able to spend as much time with my best friend."

"You were able to stay friends though," Mr. Finch noted.

"It was hard initially. Cora was married and I was a single college girl." Jill sipped from her mug. "When we both got jobs at the same school after graduation, it was easier because we saw each other every day."

"Did you and your husband socialize with the Connors?" Angie questioned.

"We did." One corner of the woman's mouth turned up. "My husband, Mitch, wasn't best friends with Richard by any stretch. They had differing views about life, but my husband was friendly with Richard because he knew it was important to me that Cora and I stay close."

"How did Richard like Mitch?" Jenna wondered if it was difficult for the couples to spend time together.

"Richard seemed to like Mitch. They never argued or anything, it was all very cordial. Like I said, Richard was sort of hard to know. He never talked about his past, was sort of stand-offish. It always seemed like he was holding back, like he really didn't care to be friends with us."

"Perhaps," said Mr. Finch, "Mr. Connors's reservation with people was due to his difficult upbringing. The man may have a hard time trusting and connecting with others."

"Cora told you about Richard's childhood?" Jill looked carefully from one to other.

Angie nodded. "She did. Just the basic facts. Not many details."

"That's because Cora doesn't know many details." Jill shook her head. "I've never met anyone like Richard. The man says nothing about his past. Nothing. It was like he arrived on the planet right before he went to college." Leaning back against the sofa, Jill's face scrunched up in thought. "You'd think he'd say something, a tiny thing, about an experience he had, a friend he knew, somewhere he visited. Nothing. I'm not even sure where he went to high school." Letting out a chuckle, she added, "Richard should have been a government spy because he would never, ever have given up any state secrets." Jill's eyes went wide. "Maybe he *was* a spy." She grunted. "I never thought of that."

"What *do* you know about Richard?" Angie asked.

"Probably as much as you know." Jill brushed at her bangs. "He moved around a lot. His mother was a drug addict. He was in foster care for years."

"I wonder why he was never adopted?" Jenna pondered.

Jill tilted her head to the side, a sad expression on her face. "I don't think Richard went into the foster care system until he was around twelve or thirteen. Back then, most people wanted to adopt a baby or a young child, not a teenager."

Mr. Finch rubbed the top of his cane. "Our early years certainly impact our adult lives, don't they."

Angie glanced at the older man sitting beside

her, sure that he was recalling his own terrible older brother who not only stole from Finch, but tried to kill him. She placed her hand on Finch's arm and gave a squeeze.

Hoping to get some additional information about the Connors family, Angie asked Jill a question. "Did your families socialize? Do you know Cora's sons well?"

Jill didn't say anything for a few moments. "We did quite a bit with the kids when they were young. Richard didn't like the beach so Cora and I and our kids would go away for long weekends together. It worked out because my husband could never get much time off. Cora's boys are a couple of years older than my son and daughter."

Angie sensed some unease coming from Jill. "Did your kids get along well?"

"You know how kids are. They got along great when they were little. When they got older, they developed different interests and went their separate ways."

"What do you think of Roman and Karl?" Jenna watched Jill's face.

Jill chose her words carefully. "Roman's a hard worker. Karl hasn't found himself yet."

Angie pushed the woman a bit with her next question. "Has Karl ever been in trouble?"

Jill's eyebrows shot up and she pursed her lips. "What did Cora tell you?"

Angie gave a shrug. "She just told us that Karl is

having a hard time finding a good job."

Jill nodded and it didn't seem like she would add anything else so Angie asked, "How did Karl get along with his father?"

"Like a lot of young men and their dads ... he chafed at Richard's expectations, he rebelled somewhat at his parents' direction."

"How so?" Finch's voice was gentle.

Jill clutched her hands together in her lap. "Karl didn't put a lot of time into his studies. He hung out with some kids that his parents didn't like. I think he took some drugs."

"What about Roman? Did he get along with his father?" Angie asked.

Jill let out a sigh. "Where Karl is a rebel, Roman is the opposite. Roman is someone who wants to please, so much so that I wonder if everything he does is just to get his father's attention and make him happy."

Angie made eye contact with Jill. "I know that our questions can seem intrusive, but Cora asked us to help and in order to figure this out, we have to ask some things that seem like none of our business. If people aren't upfront with us, then we won't be able to find any answers." The young woman paused for a moment to let her words sink in. "We need to ask you about Cora and Richard. How was their relationship?"

Jill swallowed. "I think everything was fine. I don't have any reason to believe that Richard strayed. He was always either working, running, or at home."

"Was Cora happy?" Jenna asked.

"I think so."

"You were against the relationship at first." Mr. Finch adjusted his glasses. "Did you change your mind about it as time passed?"

Jill moved her hand in the air and forced a smile. "Oh, you know. Your best friend and your kids ... they just about always choose someone you wouldn't have chosen for them." She gave a little shrug of her shoulder. "But it's not your decision ... you accept their choices."

"You didn't think that Richard was right for Cora?" Jenna asked.

"I always thought she should be with someone more fun, more social. Cora was always going out, enjoying other people's company. She was involved with so many clubs at school. Until she met Richard. Cora is more reserved around Richard." Still clutching her hands together, Jill chuckled. "It's no big deal. Cora probably thinks I should have chosen a different husband than the man I married."

Angie glanced at her sister and then looked at Jill. "What do you think happened to Richard?"

Jill blinked, her eyes wide, surprised by the directness of the question. "I...." She looked down at her hands.

Angie, Jenna, and Finch waited.

Looking at each one of her guests, Jill shook her head. "I have no idea."

"Is it possible that it might have something to do with drugs?" Jenna used a soft tone of voice. "If Karl was involved with the wrong guys ... maybe someone came looking for Karl. Maybe when Karl wasn't home, the guy got into an argument with Richard?"

Jill's eyes seemed to mist over. "Maybe. I don't know."

Jenna asked, "Do you know who Karl hung around with?"

"No." Jill shook her head. "I have no idea."

"Do you think Mr. Connors left of his own accord?" Mr. Finch looked over the tops of his glasses.

"I suppose it's possible." Jill's eyes shifted around the room. "I know that I've been around Richard for years, but honestly? I feel like I just don't know him at all." Jill shook her head. "Not at all."

CHAPTER 15

The four sisters wore ski jackets, wool hats, and gloves as they trudged up Beach Street against the cold wind. Tired of being cooped up indoors, they decided to take a walk along the sand at the edge of the ocean to have some time outside in the fresh air. It was hard to believe that in just a few months, tourists would return in droves to their little seaside village to enjoy the warm days, beautiful beaches, shops, restaurants, and museums.

Except for two people walking their dogs, the Roselands were the only hearty souls braving the cold to stroll along the long stretch of white sand beside the crashing waves. The sun had finally broken through and the high cloud cover had dissipated just in time for an hour of bright blue sky before the yellow-orange ball began its descent and hid behind the world for another winter night.

Courtney had done cartwheels along the beach while her sisters chased each other and, laughing, pretended to push one another into the waves.

"It felt good to run around outside." Courtney

removed her hat and shook some sand out of the folds. "I can't wait for spring."

Ellie eyed Jenna and smiled. "Since the carriage house is almost ready, will the spring bring a wedding to the Roseland household?"

Jenna's blue eyes sparkled. "It just might."

"Really?" Angie hugged her twin sister and then her expression turned serious. "Shouldn't we be planning things by now?"

Jenna looped her arm through Angie's. "Tom and I are going to finalize the wedding date very soon. Then we can start planning. We thought it would be nice to have an outside ceremony and a small reception, maybe on the grounds of the resort."

Courtney whooped with delight. "Now I really can't wait for spring."

Entering the Victorian, they found Mr. Finch sitting on the sofa watching a crime show in the family room with a cat curled up on each side of him. "How was your walk?"

"It was great." Courtney, her eyes glued to the television, sat down next to Euclid and the orange boy stretched and flicked his plume over her lap before resting his head back on Finch's leg. "What's in this episode? What's the crime?"

Finch explained what had happened during the first part of the hour-long show and everyone watched the last ten minutes together before moving to the kitchen to prepare pasta, grilled asparagus, and dessert for dinner. Two slow-cookers, one with a beef stew and the other with a veggie lentil bolognese, had been filled and turned on earlier in the day so that the meals would simmer for several hours. A heavenly aroma floated on the air in the kitchen causing mouths to water and stomachs to growl.

Courtney and Finch stood at the island counter mixing ingredients into two large bowls. Finch was preparing lemon drop cookies and Courtney was making a lemon meringue pie. "I've had a craving for something lemony."

Finch smiled. "Well, Miss Courtney, your craving will soon be satisfied."

At the side counter, Angie mixed together ingredients for some honey cakes that she planned to serve in the bake shop the next morning. Jenna prepared some pasta and Ellie washed and trimmed the asparagus.

"Since we're all together, let's talk about your trip to Mill City to see Cora's best friend," Ellie said.

"I'm sorry I couldn't go." Courtney passed the container of flour to Mr. Finch. "It sounded like a lot of information came out of the meeting."

Angie sighed as she mixed the ingredients with a wooden spoon. "The whole thing left me feeling anxious and uneasy. I understand that Richard Connors had a terrible early life and I get that he doesn't want to talk about it, but the lack of good information about him makes me feel like the man is a ghost."

"Speaking of ghosts...." Jenna eyed Finch and told him about the spirit that seemed to be living in her and Tom's house.

Finch raised his eyebrows and tilted his head to look over his black glass frames. "How interesting. You think the spirit is Katrina Stenmark?"

Euclid and Circe trilled from their perch on top of the fridge.

Jenna smiled at the cats. "The felines and the human sisters are in agreement that it's most likely Katrina. Stirring the water, butter, and seasonings in the pot on the stove, she cocked her head to the side. "But why is she there? Why hasn't she moved on?"

Finch formed small balls from his dough and placed them on the cookie sheet. "Perhaps, Ms. Katrina has some unfinished business."

The sisters stopped what they were doing and stared at Finch.

"What do you mean?" Ellie's blue eyes were like saucers. "Are Jenna and Tom in danger?"

"I don't believe there's any danger." Finch dusted his palms with some flour. "Didn't the woman die in that house?"

Jenna's mouth dropped open. "I'd forgotten about that." She turned the heat down so that the rice would simmer. "Maybe I deliberately forgot that detail."

"When we found out about Katrina, it was in the

middle of the necklace issue and the carriage house fire." Angie spooned some batter into muffin tins. "It sort of got lost in all that was going on."

Courtney rolled out the pie crust. "Not only did she die in that house, it sounded like she was murdered by someone who wanted that necklace."

Ellie's hand flew to her chest and she groaned. "Katrina gave her life to protect that necklace." Making eye contact with Jenna, she added, "No wonder the woman is still living in your house."

"Gosh." Jenna sat down on one of the stools at the kitchen island and placed her chin in her hand. "I really pushed that out of my head."

Finch held his cane in one hand and carried the cookie sheet to one of the ovens as he nodded to Jenna. "Well, time will tell if Ms. Katrina needs something from you or if she just needs more time to cross over due to the circumstances of her death." Finch put the cookie sheet on the oven rack and set the timer. "In the meantime, we need to discuss Richard Connors and his disappearance."

"I think we should look more closely into Karl's background and what he's up to." Jenna folded her arms and leaned on the counter. "Cora's friend suggested that he might be mixed up with drugs. One of Karl's cohorts might have come looking for him that day and had a run-in with Richard, maybe killing the man."

"It's certainly possible." Ellie placed the asparagus stalks on the grilling pan. "From what you've told me, I doubt that Richard took off with another woman, but I wonder if he'd decided to leave the family and had been preparing for a long time, maybe squirreling away money for years and getting documents ready like a false driver's license, passport, and credit cards. His disappearance is so neat and clean. The police had no leads, nothing led anywhere. Richard Connors vanished into thin air."

Courtney piped up. "Like Chief Martin said, you can't make a person stay home and you can't make a person return home. Maybe Richard doesn't want to be found, plain and simple."

Angie had been quietly considering everyone's comments and ideas. "Something bothers me about this whole mess. I suppose there's no crime if someone wants to take off. Cora has a good job and can support herself. The man's children are grown. It's a terrible thing to do, to put his family through so much worry, not to mention all the police resources that went into the investigation. So if Richard took off, he might be responsible for paying the police back for what it cost the department, but there is no criminal intent if he ran away."

Courtney and Mr. Finch, the crime show experts agreed. "That's all true."

"But...." Angie folded her arms over her chest. "We can't yet rule out foul play."

"So we'll continue with our investigation?"

Jenna asked.

"I think we have to." Angie's eyebrows scrunched together. "Something bothers me about what Cora's friend said to us about not even knowing where Richard went to high school." Angie rubbed her arms. "I get feelings of unease whenever I play that over in my head. I think there's a clue buried somewhere in there."

Nodding, Courtney poured the pie filling into the crust. "I'll go see if Cora is around and I'll ask her where Richard went to high school and when he graduated."

"Then we can look up old yearbooks for information on Richard." Finch made himself a cup of tea and sat next to Jenna at the counter. As Courtney was leaving the kitchen, Finch said, "There's something that's been bothering me about Ms. Cora."

At Mr. Finch's words, Courtney halted and turned around to hear what the older man had to say. The three other young women trained their gaze on Finch.

"What is it, Mr. Finch?" Ellie asked. "What's bothering you?"

"I've been wondering why Ms. Cora is staying here at the bed and breakfast. Her home is only an hour away. Why not drive up here whenever there's the need? Why stay at the B and B for so many days?" Finch paused and raised an eyebrow. "Does she not feel safe at home?"

Just as a cold shiver ran down Angie's back, Euclid and Circe each let out long, low growls.

CHAPTER 16

The family could hear the earsplitting voice of Mel Abel and some of the B and B guests chatting in the dining room so they brought their dinners into the family room where they could talk and eat in private.

"How can that man be so loud?" Jenna placed a hand over one of her ears pretending to try to block out what sounded like Mel booming through a megaphone.

"His friends must all have gone deaf." Courtney rolled her eyes.

When they were all settled with their meals, the discussion returned to why Cora felt the need to stay at the B and B even though she only lived an hour away.

Ellie sat in one of the easy chairs with her plate balanced on her lap. "Mr. Finch poses an excellent question. Why does Cora feel the need to stay here? Is there some reason she doesn't want to be at home?"

"Schools are back in session. Winter breaks are

over," Jenna observed. "Why isn't she in Mill City at her teaching job?"

"We'll need to ask her." Courtney had taken portions from both the veggie bolognese and the beef stew. "This veggie bolognese is delicious. Maybe I need to go vegetarian like Angie."

Angie raised an eyebrow and gave her youngest sister a look of disbelief that she would consider giving up her meat-eating ways. She made eye contact with Courtney. "Tomorrow I'd like to drive down to Mill City and talk to Karl again. Since Karl seems to be a fan of yours, you might want to sit this visit out."

"With pleasure." Courtney groaned. Going to see leering Karl again was not high on her list of priorities. "I'll do anything else to help, but I'd be happy to avoid Karl."

"What are some reasons that Cora might not want to be at home right now?" Angie asked the group.

Finch rubbed his chin. "She may feel threatened by Mr. Karl."

"Why now?" Angie pressed.

Mr. Finch continued, "Her unease could be unrelated to her husband's disappearance. Mr. Karl may be involved with drugs or the young man and his mother are at odds right now because of his lack of ambition and because he is living in her house."

"I wonder if Cora feels anxious over something

that Karl let slip about his father." Angie was trying to come up with different scenarios. "The recent use of Richard's credit card probably got the two of them talking in earnest about the disappearance again. If Karl did have something to do with his father going missing, he could have said something that caused Cora to suspect him."

Jenna sat at her desk eating from her dinner plate and tapping at her laptop at the same time. Staring at the screen, she sat upright and blinked. "Guess what? I've been looking through online Mill City high school yearbooks. Richard isn't in any of the ones you'd associate with his age. I've even looked forward from what should have been his graduation date in case it took him longer to finish high school. He isn't in any of these high school yearbooks."

"Cora wasn't around when I went to ask her where her husband went to high school," Courtney reported.

"Cora did say he went to high school in Mill City, right?" Ellie asked.

"That's what she said." Angie nodded and walked to the desk to look over Jenna's shoulder. "Maybe Cora is wrong."

"How many high schools are in Mill City?" Finch wiped his lips on his napkin.

"Three." Jenna scanned the last yearbook. "Nothing in this one either."

Angie looked at Mr. Finch. "Maybe we should

stop by the high schools tomorrow morning on our way to talk to Karl."

Finch nodded. "We can pose as freelance journalists doing a follow-up story on the missing man and explain that we wish to confirm that Richard Connors attended high school in Mill City."

"Perfect." Ellie went to the side table for a second helping of food. "I'd like to go along with you tomorrow. Jenna will be here working in her jewelry studio. She can help the guests if they need anything."

"You want to go with them?" Courtney eyed Ellie suspiciously. "Why?"

Ellie sat down again in the chair. "I want to help. Is that so strange?"

"In these cases, yes, it is." Courtney chuckled.

"Well," Ellie sniffed. "I'm trying to be less of a wimp."

"We'd be glad to have you." Angie smiled. "We should leave as early as we can. I'd like to be home by 1pm to take care of things in the bake shop. I don't want to leave everything to Louisa."

Jenna turned away from her laptop. "Someone should talk to Cora. Ask her about the things we've been wondering about."

Courtney ran her hand over Euclid's fur and eyed Angie. "I elect Angie."

"Why me?" Angie protested.

"Because." The corner of Courtney's mouth turned up. "You have the most finesse."

Angie groaned and stood up. "I better go find her." Eyeing the two felines resting on the sofa between Courtney and Finch, she added, "Maybe the cats will come with me."

Euclid gave the honey-blonde a dirty look, but he stood and stretched and jumped off the sofa with Circe following behind him.

***

After being directed by Mel Abel, Angie and the cats headed for the sunroom to find Cora. "That is one quiet woman," Mel had bellowed and pointed across the foyer to where Cora was most likely to be found. Sitting around the dining table, Mel and Orla and two other guests were engaged in a serious game of cards.

"Where's Jenna?" Orla looked up from the cards she was holding in her hands.

"She's having her dinner." Angie wondered why Orla was interested in where her Jenna was.

Cora was reading quietly by the window when the two cats and Angie entered the sunroom. Cora lifted her head from her book.

"May I sit with you?" Angie asked.

Cora nodded. "Do you have news?"

"No, but I'd like to talk with you if you're up to it." The cats jumped up on the white couch and snuggled next to Angie.

"Of course." Cora closed her book and set it

aside on the table.

"It seems that Richard might not have attended high school in Mill City." Angie looked directly at Cora to watch her reaction. "Do you have any idea where he might have gone to school?"

Cora's eyes narrowed, but her face remained neutral. "He went to high school in Mill City. It was South High."

"Do you know when he graduated? What year was it?"

Cora clasped her hands in her lap and her brows squeezed together. "It must have been the year before I graduated." She told Angie when she'd graduated high school. "I know Richard went to a school in another city for the first half of high school."

"Could there have been an alternative program that he attended? Maybe he studied in the evenings for his GED? Maybe he had to work during the day and could only attend school at night."

Cora swallowed and glanced out the window to the dark rear yard. Her voice was barely audible. "I don't think so. Richard never mentioned anything like that."

Angie smiled and tried to act nonchalant about the questionable information that Richard had shared with his wife. "Mr. Finch and I are going to take a drive to Mill City in the morning and we'll swing by the high schools to ask about Richard."

Cora seemed to have diminished in size

shrinking back against the easy chair. She gave a slight nod.

"We'd like to talk to Karl again while we're down there."

Cora's eyebrows shot up as her eyes went wide. "Why? What do you want to talk to him about?"

Angie looked pointedly at Cora. "About Richard."

"But, what about?" Cora blubbered.

"More about the day Richard went missing. Would you tell Karl to expect us around 11am?"

Cora gave a barely perceptible nod.

"I was wondering about something." Angie tried to keep her tone even and pleasant. "Are you not teaching this term?"

Cora blinked a few times. "I took some personal leave time."

"You don't have to stay here with us, you know." Angie spoke gently. "We can talk by phone or come down when we need to. Or you can come up for a few hours, if necessary. You don't need to be away from home. It's only an hour away."

Cora opened her mouth, but then closed it as she shrugged a shoulder. "I thought it would be helpful if I stayed."

"It's okay to go back," Angie said encouragingly. "We don't want to keep you from your job or your sons or your friends. We'll keep in touch."

"I don't mind." Cora gave a weak smile.

Angie leaned slightly forward and asked in a

kind voice, "Is there a reason you don't want to be home right now?"

"What? No. Everything's fine ... I mean, nothing's fine, but there's no reason," Cora stammered.

The cats lifted their heads and glanced at Angie.

Angie could feel that Cora was holding something back and the sensation caused a chill to run through her blood. "Has Karl been difficult to have at home?"

Cora forced a chuckle. "Aren't all adult children difficult to live with?"

Angie ignored the statement and asked the next question. "Is Karl involved with drugs?"

"No." Cora shook her head with vigor.

"What about his friends? Are they involved with drugs?"

Cora bit her lower lip. "I don't know. I don't think so."

Angie decided to be direct. "Are you afraid to be at home right now?"

Cora's hand flew up to her throat like a fluttering bird, but she shook her head and forced another chuckle. "Of course not." Glancing at her watch, Cora reached for her book from the table. "Everything's fine." She nodded for emphasis. "If you don't mind, I'd like to head up to my room now. I'll talk to you tomorrow." The woman walked quickly out of the sunroom leaving Angie and the two cats sitting on the sofa.

Looking at her feline companions, Angie sighed. "Everything's *not* fine and there *is* a reason that Cora doesn't want to be at home right now."

Euclid and Circe growled low in their throats.

Angie looked towards the sunroom doorway. "But the question is ...what is that reason?"

CHAPTER 17

Parked in the visitor lot of one of the Mill City high schools, Ellie sat in the driver's seat of her van with Angie in the back and Finch sitting in the front passenger seat. They had just come out of the third and last high school in Mill City. Snow flurries fluttered down and gathered over the windshield wipers. Ellie and Finch perched in their seats so that they could see Angie behind them as they discussed the early morning visits to the schools.

The three had been welcomed by the office staffers who, before running some reports on their computers trying to locate Richard Connors's records, explained that due to privacy laws, they could only confirm the man's attendance and could not provide any details about his grades or courses taken.

Nothing came up indicating that the man had gone to any of the schools. The secretaries pulled out yearbooks from the time the man was supposed to be in attendance, but like Jenna's investigation, they came up empty. "If he attended school here," the secretaries declared, "he would be listed as a graduate in the yearbook."

"So what do you make of it?" Ellie pulled her gloves on while looking from Finch to Angie.

"Mr. Connors was not a student at any of these high schools, despite what he told his wife." Finch looked out the window at the sprawling, one-level school. "Either Cora misunderstood or the man lied to his wife."

Angie sighed. "What's going on here? Why would Richard hide where he went to school? If he didn't graduate from high school, then how did he get into college?"

"Who knows?" Ellie adjusted in her seat and turned the key in the ignition. "Let's go talk to Karl."

In less than fifteen minutes, the amateur sleuths were sitting in Cora Connors's living room. Karl, unshaven and with mussed hair, slouched in his seat, his legs dangling over the arm of the chair. His bare feet stuck out from the bottom of his jeans.

"Did your mother forget to tell you we were coming?" Ellie sat straight.

"Naw. She told me. I forgot to set the alarm." Karl yawned and rubbed his eyes.

"Late night?" Angie smiled trying to make Karl comfortable.

Karl only shrugged. "What's this visit about? Didn't we cover everything last time?"

The smile faded from Angie's face. She could see

141

how Karl would be a pain to have living in the house. "What do you know about your father's credit card that was recently used for several purchases?"

"Nothing. Like what?"

"Like why wasn't that card cancelled when your father went missing?"

Karl shrugged again. "I don't know."

"Did your father carry an emergency credit card with him?" Ellie stared with distaste at the slovenly mess before them.

"That's what my mom said."

"Mr. Karl, we'd appreciate it if you'd take our questions seriously." Mr. Finch held his cane between his knees and Angie could see by the look on his face that he might want to give Karl a smack with it.

"I am." Karl nearly whined.

Angie used an official sounding voice. "You understand that we are not law enforcement? We are only consultants for the police department." She paused. "You won't get into trouble by answering my next question honestly. Do you hang around with or know anyone involved with the buying or selling of drugs?"

Karl lifted his head and smirked. "Yeah."

Angie asked. "Were any of those people angry with you over something at the time of your father's disappearance?"

"I don't think so."

"Karl, we're trying to help find out what happened to your dad." Ellie narrowed her eyes and spoke softly. "Any little thing could lead to a clue. Was anyone annoyed with you at the time?"

"Possibly." Karl swung his legs from the arm of the chair and placed his feet on the floor. He yawned again.

"Could you ever imagine that someone you know could do something terrible when in a rage? Could they lose their temper and beat someone up?"

Karl ran his hand over his hair. "Sure."

"Who?" Ellie wanted names.

Karl snorted. "Everyone I know."

Angie leaned forward trying to make eye contact with Karl. "What do you think happened to your father? You must have a theory."

A cloud covered the young man's face. "You want to know what I think? I think dear old Dad took off, left us, skedaddled. I bet he planned it for years. I bet he siphoned off money into another account. He was the one who handled the bills, Mom wouldn't have known. I bet he got falsified documents under another name, a driver's license, a passport. I'm only surprised that he left his precious shoes behind. They were more important to him than we were." Karl's jaw tightened. "You want to know what I think? I think good riddance, glad you're gone, Dad, don't let the door hit you on the way out. That's what I think." Karl stood up, his fists clenched. "I need coffee." He left the room without asking the guests if they wanted anything.

Ellie blinked as she watched the young man leave the living room. "So, is the interview over?"

Angie's heart was pounding as she let out a breath. "No, it isn't. If he doesn't come back, we'll join him in the kitchen." She looked at Mr. Finch. "We might want to take this time to stretch our legs."

"Indeed." Mr. Finch gave a wink and stood up with a slight smile on his face. "Perhaps, I will seek out the rest room."

Angie walked slowly around the room, glancing at objects, checking out the book shelves, quietly opening drawers.

Ellie's mouth was hanging open. She flicked her eyes to the hall to see if Karl was returning. "What are you doing?" she whispered. "Don't open their drawers."

Angie frowned. "There has to be a clue around here. Stand up, Ellie. Walk around. See if you sense anything. I'm going to look in Richard's office. If Karl comes back, tell him we went to use the bathroom."

Ellie jumped to her feet. "Oh. Don't do that. Don't get caught. I don't trust this guy. Don't anger him."

"Too late, he's already angry." Angie touched her sister gently on the arm. "Walk around in here. Try to pick up on anything. Don't let Karl scare you." She winked. "There are three of us and only

144

one of him ... and one of *us* has a cane."

"Angie, don't go snooping around." Ellie's voice shook.

Angie said gently, "You said you wanted to help. Take some deep breaths. Karl won't hurt us. Open your mind to the energies in this house. Try to feel something. I'll be right back."

Ellie gave a reluctant nod of her head as her sister headed out of the living room into the hall.

Her heart pounding, Angie hurried away to Richard's small office at the back of the house trying to walk as quietly as possible, all the while looking over her shoulder to see if Karl had left the kitchen and was making his return to the living room. Turning the knob on the closed door, she entered and quickly shut the door behind her, breathing out a sigh of relief.

Angie ran her hands over the desk, picked up the pens and pencils, opened the desk drawers, and touched her fingers to papers and file folders. Anything of interest had been removed by the police, but Angie tried closing her eyes and opening her senses to what might have lingered behind. Picking up a blue folder, she flipped through the papers and stopped short as she stared at a bill from an attorney in Mill City addressed to Cora. For a moment, the letters on the page seemed to glow and Angie had to snap her eyes shut as something picked at her with a low-energy buzz.

She froze in place when she heard Karl and Mr.

Finch at the other end of the hall.

"I needed to use the rest room," Mr. Finch spoke. "May I have a cup of tea, if you don't mind?" Angie knew that Finch was trying to herd Karl back to the kitchen so that she could make her escape from the office. When she heard them retreating, she slipped from the room and hustled quietly back to the living room where she took a seat.

"I almost died waiting for you." Ellie's face was pale and her voice breathless. "Karl was almost back here, but Mr. Finch took him into the kitchen. Can we leave? I don't like it in this house."

"Soon." Angie turned when she heard Karl apologize that there weren't any tea bags in the cupboard. The men entered the room, Karl clutching a coffee mug.

"So are we done here?" Karl looked to Angie.

"Almost." Angie smiled and nodded. "Just a few more questions."

Letting out a loud sigh, Karl sat down. "What else do you want to know?"

"Do you know much about your father's background? Where he grew up? Where he went to school?"

Karl dipped his chin and glared at Angie. "He had a tough upbringing. He went to the state college here in Mill City. He never talked about his life and we weren't encouraged to ask questions."

Angie had an idea. "How old is your father?"

"A year older than my mom."

146

A scurry of unease shot through Angie's body. "Are your mother's parents still living?"

"Yeah. I don't see much of them. They live in Gloucester." Karl scowled. "You planning to pester them next?"

"May I remind you that we are looking into your father's disappearance at your mother's request." Ellie held Karl's eyes.

Angie asked, "Can you think of any reason why your mother might not feel safe here at home?"

An expression of alarm washed over Karl's face. "She doesn't feel safe?"

"I didn't say that." Angie placed her hands in her lap. "I'm asking if there might be some reason she would be uncomfortable staying at home right now."

Karl's eyes darted around the room. "No. Why would she be uncomfortable here?"

Angie glanced at her sister and Finch. "I guess that's all for now. If you think of anything that might help, just give us a call." She stood and thanked the young man and the three interrogators left the house. Mr. Finch held Ellie's arm as they walked to the van.

"Something is not right in that house." Mr. Finch moved carefully over the spots of ice on the walkway. "I can feel it."

"Yes." Angie took a quick look back at the house as she opened the van door. "So can I."

CHAPTER 18

Angie had just put a honey cake in the oven and was wiping down the tables in the bake shop when Jenna came in from the door that linked the shop with the commercial side of the Victorian's kitchen.

Jenna made herself a hot tea and sat at the counter. "I finished some new designs for the summer line. I'm happy with how they're coming out. I'll show you later." After taking a sip from her cup, she set it down and looked at Angie. "I'm dying to hear what happened on your visit to Mill City, but first I want to tell you what happened when I went over to my house this morning."

Angie came to stand by the counter and looked at Jenna with interest.

"Courtney went off to the candy store and I was going to work on my designs while watching the B and B for Ellie. I realized I'd left my sketch book at my house so I hurried over to pick it up." Jenna put her chin in her hand and leaned on the counter top. "The sketch book wasn't where I left it."

Angie's mouth opened. "The ghost?"

"I prefer to call her Katrina." Jenna nodded. "I had the sensation I was being watched. I hunted all over the downstairs rooms for my book, but I couldn't find it."

"What happened?"

"I heard something fall over upstairs. Just like last time. I went upstairs and into the library. The sketchbook had been neatly placed on the small desk by the window. That photograph of Katrina, her husband, and son was sitting right next to my book."

"Huh." Angie stared at her sister. "What do you make of it?"

Jenna sighed and chuckled. "I have no idea."

"Are you worried? Do you feel threatened?"

"Not at all." Picking up her teacup, she said, "It's just going to be weird having a third person in the house with us."

"What does Tom say?"

Jenna laughed. "He said he's going to charge Katrina rent for living there."

The corner of Angie's mouth turned up as she checked the honey cake in the oven. "Well, having a ghost around might be like having a built-in security system in the house."

Jenna just shook her head. "Tell me about the trip to Mill City."

Angie gave Jenna all the details of the trip to the Mill City high schools and their stop to see Karl. She let out a sigh. "When we started on this case, I thought it was going to be straightforward. We look into it, a decent man is missing, the credit card was used by someone else, we don't find anything more than what the police found, and that's it. Now we wonder if Richard Connors might have gone missing on purpose."

"But...." Jenna raised an eyebrow. "Some weird things have poked their heads up."

"Yes. Things that toss the case into a different light." Angie leaned on the counter across from her sister. "I think Cora doesn't want to be at home right now. It seems Richard didn't attend the high school he claimed to graduate from. Karl is full of rage for his father. And there was a bill for an attorney's visit addressed to Cora in Richard's desk. The bill was dated at the end of last August, shortly before Richard's disappearance."

"How does it all connect? What are we missing?" Jenna's face was serious.

"When I went into Richard's office and shuffled though the papers and folders, I could feel little electric shocks in my fingers. I found the attorney's bill and was about to look through more of the papers when I heard Mr. Finch talking to Karl at the end of the hall. I didn't have time to scan the other paperwork, I had to get back to the living room, but some of the things in the folder were Richard's passport, his birth certificate, a scanned copy of his driver's license. Everyday things like that. I don't know what it means."

"It must be pointing to something." Jenna shook her head. "From the beginning, Ellie's thought that Richard is alive."

"She must be right." Angie picked up a cloth and absent-mindedly ran it over the top of the counters. "But Karl worries me. Is his rage so great that he hurt his father?" She shook her head. "I think we need to talk to Cora's parents. I'll bet they have some insight into Richard that only in-laws would have. I also think that we should pay a visit to Robin's Point. When I was down there the other night at the resort with Josh, I felt calm and close to Nana. Walking around the Point might clear our heads and help us connect the dots on this case."

Jenna agreed. "We'll get everyone together and head down there. Hopefully we don't freeze to death as we walk around."

The door to the bake shop opened and Chief Martin entered the store. He brushed some snow flakes from his shoulders and removed his cap. "Afternoon." Taking a seat on the stool next to Jenna, he took a long swig of the coffee Angie brought him.

Angie eyed the chief. "You have some news?"

The chief had a manila envelope that he opened. Removing several photographs, he spread them over the counter. "These are the enhanced photos from the video camera in the New Hampshire motel you visited. Take a look."

Angie and Jenna lifted the photos and inspected

them.

"It could be Richard." Angie brought one picture close to her face.

"It could also be someone else." Jenna put down the photograph she'd been holding. "What do the police say?"

"The same thing you both just said. Inconclusive." Chief Martin raised his mug. "Why don't these cameras produce better film?" He shook his head. "They're for security purposes, for Pete's sake. What good is the security if the photos are too blurred and grainy to make out anyone's features?"

"Have you shown them to Cora?" Angie filled the sugar bowl on the counter.

"I'm on my way. I wanted to show them to you first."

Angie could feel agitation coming off the chief and it flooded her with unease. "You have something else to tell us?"

Jenna swiveled on her stool to better face the chief.

"You know that Mill City psychic that consulted on the case?" Chief Martin's shoulders sagged. "He told the police that he thought Richard Connors would be or had recently been in Mill City."

Angie's eyebrows shot up.

"What?" Jenna sat up straighter.

The chief gave a nod.

Angie's voice was nearly a whisper. "Richard in

Mill City?"

The chief gave the girls a frown. "It might be worth your while to pay a visit to the psychic's wife."

Angie and Jenna reported their recent findings and suspicions to the chief and he rubbed his chin. "There's more going on here than meets the eye."

The bake shop door opened again and in walked Cora Connors. "Hello. Are you closed? Ellie told me that you might have some of those fruit squares here in the shop that we had for evening snacks yesterday."

Angie smiled. "The shop is closed for the day, but it doesn't matter." She eyed the chief. "Lots of people come in after closing. We still have some of the fruit squares." Angie moved to the display case. "How many would you like?"

Cora edged over to the case. "Two, please, one blueberry and one raspberry."

Jenna slipped the photographs from the motel video camera into a pile and tucked them into the envelope. She and the chief made eye contact.

"No time like the present, I guess." Chief Martin picked up the envelope and walked over to Cora just as Angie handed the woman a small bakery box.

"Mrs. Connors, I have some photos to show you from the security camera in New Hampshire. I was about to go find you in the Victorian."

Cora's eyes widened and a look of apprehension

153

spread over her face. Chief Martin explained the condition of the photos and that the determination of whether or not it was actually her husband in the pictures was inconclusive. "Would you be able to take a look?"

Cora gave the tiniest of nods as she clutched the brown box that contained her fruit squares.

The chief gestured to a table across the room by the windows. "Would you like to sit down here or would you prefer to go somewhere else?"

"You can sit in the sunroom inside," Angie offered.

"Here is fine." Cora stared at the envelope in the Chief's hand.

Angie could see some tears glistening in the corners of Cora's eyes.

"I'll lock up." Jenna headed to the bake shop door, turned the bolt, and flipped over the small rectangular sign that said, 'Closed.'

Busying themselves with the end of the day tasks, Angie and Jenna worked at the end of the bake shop away from Cora and the chief who sat huddled at the table with their backs to the girls.

"I wonder what she'll think." Jenna walked past her sister as she carried a tray of dirty dishes to the dishwasher inside the house.

Angie wondered the very same thing. Ideas and bits of what they'd found out swirled around in her head so fast, she almost felt dizzy. Did Cora want it to be Richard in the photos? Why does the woman seem reluctant to go home? Is Richard dead or alive? Did Karl have something to do with his father's disappearance? Why did Richard lie about where he'd attended high school? *Why did I feel those little shocks in my fingers when I picked up some of the papers in Richard's office?*

Angie's head snapped up when she heard Cora let out a little gasp. The woman had her hand at her throat. Bending close to the photos, she shuddered. "It could be. I think it is. I think it *is* Richard." She stood up so fast that the legs of her chair made a loud screeching sound on the wood floor. Fumbling with the lock, Cora flung the door open and rushed from the bake shop with tears running down her face. She left the bakery box on the table.

The door of the bake shop banged so hard against the jamb that it flew open again. Walking to shut and lock it, Angie looked over to the chief who was coming towards her carrying Cora's box of squares in one hand and the manila envelope in the other.

"Poor woman." Chief Martin handed the box to Angie. "She's been through a lot." He looked down at the envelope. "I can't say I agree with her assessment of the photos. She sure got emotional."

Angie held the chief's eyes. "But were those tears of shock and happiness ... or of fear?"

CHAPTER 19

Angie carried the bakery box as she checked for Cora in the dining room and living room before finding her sitting at the far end of the sunroom staring out the windows. She leapt to her feet when she heard Angie enter the room.

"Oh!" Cora's hand covered her chest. "It's you." The woman's tears were gone, but her cheeks were flushed and the rims of her eyelids were tinged pink.

Angie spoke in a soft voice as she set the brown box on the table next to where Cora had been sitting. "Sorry to startle you. You left the squares behind in the bake shop."

"Thank you." Cora slumped into the chair. "I shouldn't have run off. I'm embarrassed that I left Chief Martin like that." The woman's face was wrinkled and drawn causing her to look ten years older than when she arrived at the Victorian.

Angie took the seat opposite. "It's okay. He understands. You've been through quite a lot."

Cora gave a slight nod and looked down at her

hands. Euclid and Circe came into the room and jumped up onto the white sofa.

"You think that it's Richard in the photos?"

"I thought one of the pictures looked like him." Cora's lower lip trembled. "It surprised me to see Richard. I felt overcome." She rubbed at the corners of her eyes.

Brushing her hand over her face, Cora went on, her words rushing out in a torrent. "Everything just came to a head. All my questions seemed to be drowning me. If it *is* Richard, why doesn't he just come home? What happened to him? Did someone kidnap him? Did he go off on his own? Did he plan this whole thing? Why would he do this? Is he mentally unstable? Does he need our help?" She looked like she was about to say something else, but changed her mind and turned her head to the windows, her shoulders slumped.

"Do you want him to come home?" Angie asked gently.

Cora's head whipped around. "Of course. Why wouldn't I?"

Angie answered with a soft tone of voice. "There are lots of reasons. You might feel resentment towards Richard for putting the family through this. Or maybe you're worried that he is suffering from mental illness and you're afraid you won't handle it well. Maybe you're afraid he was kidnapped and won't be the same person when he returns. It's a terrible and complicated situation. There aren't any roadmaps on how to handle something like this." Angie paused for a moment. "Have you talked to someone who might help you sort through it all?"

"You mean a psychiatrist?" Cora snapped at Angie.

"I mean a counselor or a therapist. It might help."

Cora shook her head. "You think I can't handle this."

Angie stifled a sigh. She wanted to help Cora, but was unsure how to go about it. What she'd just suggested certainly didn't go over well. "That isn't what I meant. It would be someone to talk to who isn't personally involved." Angie wanted to ask Cora about her visit to the Mill City attorney, but didn't think that Cora would appreciate the inquiry at the moment. As she looked at the woman and wondered what to say next, a sudden wave of panic washed over Angie and made her want to rush from the room. Little zips of electricity seemed to flash in the tips of her fingers.

Euclid stood up and twitched his tail back and forth.

Angie swallowed. "How old is Richard?"

A flicker of surprise at the question showed on Cora's face. "A year older than me."

"That would make him ... what?"

"Forty-five. Why do you ask?"

"You said that Richard went to high school in

Mill City. Which one did you say he went to?"

Cora cocked her head to the side. "South High."

Angie took in a slow breath. "We visited South High School this morning. They don't have a record of Richard attending."

Cora stared at Angie, her mouth hanging slightly open. After a few moments, she spoke. "They must be mistaken."

"The secretaries got some yearbooks from the school library. Richard wasn't in any of them."

Color rose in Cora's face. "So what are you implying? That Richard is a liar? That's ridiculous. Maybe he didn't submit a photo to the yearbook. Maybe they lost his records."

"Do you think Richard planned his disappearance?"

Cora's cheeks flushed bright red and she bit her lip. "Why would he do that? We had a nice life. We got along."

Angie's face was stern, her body felt flooded with unease. "If the photo from the motel is actually Richard, do you still think that he is sending you a message by using the credit card?"

"Yes. I do."

"What is the message?"

"That he's alive, of course."

Angie was about to ask another question, when Mel Abel appeared in the doorway practically filling the space with his round body. "Ladies." Mel nodded and looked at Angie. "Is your sister around? We were wondering if afternoon snacks would be out soon."

Angie stood up. "I'll go see about bringing them out."

Mel stepped back to let Angie out of the room and turned his eyes to Cora. "Why don't you join us in the dining room?"

Cora declined. "I have some reading I want to get done."

"Suit yourself." Mel followed Angie through the living room into the foyer. They heard Cora shut the glass doors leading to the sunroom. "You ladies having an argument?"

"No, it's not that." Angie rubbed at the tension in her neck. "We were discussing her missing husband. It's a difficult topic."

Mel spoke in an uncharacteristically soft voice. "It might not be so difficult if she was upfront about things."

Angie narrowed her eyes and looked at the chubby-cheeked man walking beside her. "Why do you say that?"

Mel scrunched up his face. "It's clear to anyone with sense that she's holding back. She hides from everyone in the house, goes off reading by herself, doesn't come down for breakfast until we've all cleared out. She only lives an hour away. Why is she holed up here?" Mel raised an eyebrow. "You and your sisters and old Finch are trying to help her, right?" The man leaned close to Angie.

"Somebody might be playing a game of hide and seek, and if it was me, I'd be careful about believing what she says. I wouldn't trust her." He shrugged. "Just sayin'." Mel went into the dining room and poured himself a cup of coffee.

Jolts of electricity jumped down Angie's back. "I'll see to the afternoon snacks."

***

Angie tore into the kitchen to find Ellie preparing the beverage cart with chocolate pudding cake, a variety of cookies, and fruit. Mr. Finch and Courtney were sitting at the table writing down some new ideas for fudge flavors, and Jenna and Tom were perched on stools at the kitchen island going over color cards trying to decide on a paint shade for their bedroom. Everyone looked up when Angie entered the room.

"What's wrong with you?" Jenna eyed her twin.

"I was talking to Cora." Angie, pacing around the kitchen full of nervous energy, told them what was said. "She doesn't believe that Richard ran off. She's sure the Mill City high school just can't find Richard's records of attendance. When I was talking with her, I felt electricity in my fingertips. I think it has something to do with the papers I was holding when I was in Richard's office. I think it has something to do with her visit to the Mill City attorney. I wish I could get back into that office.

Maybe Cora would take us back to the house and give me access to the office."

Ellie stood next to the snack cart listening to Angie. "Please don't try to get back in there without Cora with you. Karl is full of anger. Who knows what he might do?"

Angie downed a glass of water. "And then," she made eye contact with her family, "Mel Abel told me that he didn't think Cora was being honest with us."

"Really?" Jenna frowned. "Why would he say that?"

"He said he wouldn't trust her." Angie sat down across from Mr. Finch and Courtney. "When Mel said those words, I felt electric jolts pulsing down my back. I think he's right. I think we have to be careful about what Cora tells us."

"How would Mel know anything?" Tom asked. "Is it just a feeling he gets from Cora?"

"I think it must be." Angie rubbed the back of her neck.

"Mel sort of has a nerve saying that about Cora." Courtney scowled. "Mel doesn't know Cora. And why are these guests staying at the B and B for so long? It's winter. People don't stay here this long in the winter. These people won't leave."

The others stared at Courtney.

"Well, I'm glad they're here. It's boosting the bank account in a very slow time of year." Ellie pushed the snack cart into the hall to head for the dining room.

"Those three guests *have* been here longer than most people stay." Finch stroked his chin. "We suspect that Cora has reasons why she doesn't want to go home. What those reasons are remain to be determined. But what about the other two guests? Why are Mr. Abel and Ms. Orla staying at the B and B for so long?"

Tom shrugged. "It's winter. What else do they have to do? They're having fun here. Why is everyone so suspicious?"

Jenna turned to Tom and her eyes narrowed. "Orla is always giving me the third degree. She asks me all kinds of questions. It makes me uncomfortable ... and I find it odd."

"Why odd?" Courtney looked at Jenna with concern.

Jenna fiddled with the end of a lock of her hair. "It's like ... I don't know ... it's almost like she wants something from me."

While the family exchanged looks with one another, Tom protectively reached over and took Jenna's hand.

"What's going on around here?" Angie muttered.

CHAPTER 20

"Cora sure was annoyed with us when we wouldn't let her come on this visit." Jenna drove along the road that ran parallel to the ocean heading for the town of Gloucester.

"I don't think her parents would be forthcoming with us if Cora was sitting there while they talk to us about Richard." Angie watched the scenery pass by from the back seat.

"This should be a very interesting visit." Mr. Finch sat in the front passenger seat. "I only wish that we could have brought the cats with us."

"This is it. Here's the house." Jenna eased the car to a stop in front of a large, neat, white Cape-style house. "Ready?'

In several minutes, the Roseland twins and Mr. Finch were seated in the living room of Cora Connors's parents. A fire was burning in the fireplace, and cookies, coffee, and tea were set on the coffee table. Some general chit chat ensued before Angie asked Mr. and Mrs. Ladd the first question about their son-in-law.

"Thank you for seeing us." Angie nodded. "We thought it was important to get your perspective on Richard and his disappearance."

Mrs. Ladd was short and petite and her white hair was cut short and stylishly around her face. She held her teacup in one hand and balanced the saucer on her leg as she trained her piercing blue eyes on Angie. "I'm not sure how much help we can be."

"We'll try, of course," Mr. Ladd said. The man was tall and slender and had a full head of white hair. "What can we tell you?"

"Could you tell us what you thought about Richard?" Jenna asked. "What kind of person was he, how did you get along, things like that."

"We weren't keen on Cora marrying so young." Mr. Ladd glanced at his wife. "We thought they should wait until they graduated, get to know each other better, not rush into things."

Mrs. Ladd nodded.

"I guess they didn't take your suggestion." Mr. Finch smiled warmly at the couple. "Did you like Mr. Connors? Did you and your son-in-law get along? Did you spend time together?"

Mr. Ladd answered. "We hoped for the best. When they married, we really didn't know Richard at all. Cora and Richard lived in Mill City and we moved here so we didn't see a lot of them. Richard was cordial whenever we got together."

"Was there anything about him that you didn't

like?" Angie questioned.

Mr. Ladd chuckled. "Sure. I'd hoped to be friends with my son-in-law. You know, play some golf together, watch some sports together, maybe, get dinner on occasion. That was my fantasy. Richard didn't share my interest in doing things together." He gave a shrug. "I didn't take it personally."

Mr. Finch made eye contact with Mrs. Ladd. "What are your thoughts on Richard?"

Mrs. Ladd took a quick look at her husband as she set her teacup on the table and then clasped her hands in her lap. "I've never trusted Richard." She let her words float on the air before adding, "Not from the very beginning."

"Why not?" Angie was surprised at the woman's forthcoming comment.

Mrs. Ladd's lips were tight. "I could never put my finger on it, really. At first, I thought I was being overly critical, but something about Richard has picked at me all these years."

Finch encouraged the woman to say more. "What were your concerns?"

Mrs. Ladd let out an exasperated sigh. "Richard was always polite, cordial, conversed with us about world events, local news, his job, the kids."

Mr. Finch tilted his head in question.

"But he never talked about himself." Mrs. Ladd held her hands up. "Never."

Mr. Ladd said, "We know about Richard's

background. Cora told us. It's understandable that he wouldn't want to talk about his past."

"That still doesn't explain his complete silence about everything." Mrs. Ladd looked from Angie to Jenna to Finch as if they might offer the answer. "You'd think the man would talk about *something* he'd done as a child or a teen or a young man, but no. Nothing. He always avoided my questions. I find it very odd."

Mr. Ladd forced a smile. "I think my wife is making more of it than it requires."

"I've always sensed something was off with Richard." Mrs. Ladd shook her head, leaned forward, and used a conspiratorial tone. "I've always thought he was older than he claimed to be."

"There's no evidence for that." Mr. Ladd tilted his head.

"Richard is *not* one year older than Cora." Mrs. Ladd's face was screwed up in a pout. "He's older. I'm sure of it."

A flicker of anxiety rushed through Angie's body and she took quick looks at Jenna and Mr. Finch to see if they sensed the same thing. Jenna raised an eyebrow and Finch gave an almost imperceptible nod which told Angie that she was not alone in her feelings.

"How did Richard get along with his sons?" Jenna wanted to hear the Ladd's take on Richard's and his boys' relationship.

Mr. Ladd spoke. "Richard was a hard worker.

He expected the boys to do well in school, do some chores around the house. Richard wasn't touchy-feely with his children, he had expectations for his sons, he wanted them to work hard and be contributing citizens."

Mrs. Ladd huffed. "The man could have shown a more loving side. He was too strict. He didn't show the boys affection. Children need affection. They need to know that they are loved for who they are, not who you hope they become."

Angie liked Mrs. Ladd and was eager to hear more of her impressions. "Did the boys get along with Richard?"

Mrs. Ladd gave a shake of her head. "Roman was a pleaser. He would do anything that anyone asked him to do. Karl, on the other hand, has a rebellious streak. He'd dig in whenever Richard wanted him to do something. I think the boy wanted his father's love and when it was withheld, Karl would resist or oppose his father."

Mr. Ladd frowned at his wife. "That sounds very harsh. Some kids just chafe against parental supervision."

"And some kids don't get the attention they need." Mrs. Ladd moved her hand around for emphasis. "Oh, Cora did her best, but Karl craved his father's attention and approval. I agree that the boy is difficult. He still is to this day. But I think if Karl had been handled differently, things would have turned out differently. It's just my two cents."

"We appreciate your openness." Mr. Finch nodded. "Forgive the bluntness of my question, but has Karl had issues with drugs?"

Mr. Ladd said, "He hangs around with questionable friends. I wouldn't be surprised if he took drugs, but honestly we don't know."

"What do you think has happened to Mr. Connors?" Finch questioned.

"The police think he took off." Sadness permeated Mr. Ladd's tone. He reached over to gently take his wife's hand.

The woman swallowed hard and brushed at her bangs. "I think that Richard was irreparably harmed by his childhood. I think he is unstable, but I can't believe that he grew tired of being a family-man and just abandoned our daughter and grandsons." The woman's eyes clouded. "If he did, then God help him if he ever shows his face around me again." Shaking her head, she looked down at her hands in her lap. "I think it was foul play. I think that one day someone will find Richard and then my daughter can put this whole mess to rest." When she looked at her guests, they could see the tears gathering in her eyes. "I hope with all of my heart that you can find a tiny clue that will make a difference. Please keep trying."

Angie couldn't put her finger on it, but she knew something about their visit and what the Ladds had told them was important ... she could feel it thrumming through her blood.

CHAPTER 21

"Why do I feel so uneasy?" Angie eyed the front door of the Mill City residence that she, Jenna, Courtney, and Finch were walking towards. "I've never been around a psychic before."

Courtney gave her sister a look. "Really?" She made a circular gesture with her hand. "What about all of us?"

Angie's eyes were wide from the unease she was feeling about coming to speak with the wife of the psychic who had consulted with the police on Richard Connor's case. "I don't think of us as psychics."

A smile formed over Courtney's face as she shook her head. "I'm not sure what else you'd call us since we all have paranormal skills."

"Shh." Angie tried to shush Courtney. "Don't talk about it in public."

Courtney ignored Angie and thought for a moment. "Although, Ellie's thing is more the telekinesis stuff. I guess you could still call her a psychic though ... you know how she sometimes can tell when someone is about to call or come to the door."

The four stood on the front porch of the psychic's former home waiting for his wife to answer the doorbell.

"Could we talk about this later?" Angie adjusted her scarf against the cold wind.

Just as Jenna was about to push the button again for the doorbell, the front door opened and a short, gray-haired older woman stood in the small foyer of her home looking from person to person. "The Roselands and Mr. Finch, isn't it? I'm Melinda Carter." She had a soft, kind voice. "Please come in." Leading them to the room on the right of the foyer, she said, "I thought we could sit around the dining table and talk. I've put out coffee and tea and water and some banana bread." The dining table had been set with delicate cups and saucers, napkins, silverware, and small white plates, with carafes of coffee and tea placed in the center. "Please sit down."

"How lovely." Mr. Finch eyed the nicely set table with appreciation. "You shouldn't have gone to so much trouble."

"I'm happy to do it."

When the group was settled around the table and condolences had been offered for the loss of her husband, the older woman began the conversation. "My husband, Arthur, was a good man, a very kind person. He worked as an accountant all of his adult

J.A Whiting

life. He only retired last year, and still he did some part time work for his firm. He enjoyed keeping busy." She passed the plate of cookies to Jenna. "As you know, Arthur also had a skill. A skill he wanted to use to help others."

"Did your husband have his skill from the time he was a boy?" Finch was quite interested to hear about the man.

"He did." Melinda Carter nodded her head and smiled. "His parents frowned on such things, but his grandmother had the same ability and quietly answered Arthur's questions and helped him understand what he could do."

"When did he tell you about his gift?" Angie asked.

"He told me after we'd been dating for a while." Melinda smiled warmly. "He took a big chance revealing his skill to me. It was a brave thing to do."

"You took it well, I guess." Courtney's face was bright with interest.

"I thought it was fascinating ... and it was part of who Arthur was." Melinda paused for a moment. "For over sixty years, I loved that man and all of his wonderful qualities." Winking at her guests, she told them, "That included his *unusual* characteristics."

Courtney smiled. "Maybe your husband *sensed* that you would be open to his ... ah, interesting ability."

Melinda chuckled. "That could very well be."

"Did he consult with the police often?" Courtney wanted to hear all about Arthur's experiences.

"Unfortunately, there is no shortage of evil doers." Melinda's expression turned somber. "Arthur was called in to help fairly often. It wasn't just for Mill City. He traveled all over the country to assist the authorities. Twice he even went all the way to England."

Courtney's blue eyes sparkled. "Cool."

"You'd think that Arthur would tell me all about the incidents he was involved with, but he was bound by two restrictions. One being the confidentiality required of working with law enforcement. Details couldn't be shared, things had to be hush-hush. They certainly didn't want to alert any of the suspects if they were on to them. The second reason was a personal one ... working the cases and using all of his senses to evaluate a situation was exhausting for him. I think it took a serious toll on his health. As he got older, I often insisted that he decline the police request to consult for them." Sadness tugged at Melinda's face and a slight tremble fluttered over her lips. "Arthur's heart was weak. He'd had several heart attacks. I feared that any more 'experiences' would be fatal." Looking down at her cup, she swallowed and sighed. "I was right."

"You think he passed away because of his psychic abilities?" Jenna's eyes were sad.

"I think it was too much for him. He had a heart attack shortly after the last thing he tried to help with."

Angie said, "The police told us that your husband had contacted them recently about the Richard Connors case. Did he have new information?"

"I don't know much and I'm sorry I can't help you as much as I'd like to, but as I said, Arthur did not share details. I do know that he had very strong feelings that Richard Connors was alive and well."

"That's what he told the police? That was the newly shared information?" Mr. Finch leaned slightly forward.

"It was more than that." Melinda looked from person to person. "Arthur felt strongly that Richard was about to make a visit to Mill City or was already here."

Angie's eyes nearly bugged out of her head. "Here? In Mill City? Why?"

Melinda shook her head. "He didn't know why, but he felt that Richard's intentions were dangerous ones."

"Then the man's return is not to be celebrated." Finch rubbed his chin and looked over his eyeglass frames at the sisters. "Which suggests that Richard Connors did not meet with foul play. The man probably was not kidnapped or harmed in any way. His disappearance seems to have been self-driven."

"That is what Arthur thought from the

beginning." Melinda ran her finger over the handle of her porcelain cup. "Arthur experienced a profound sense of anxiety and concern over what he called Richard's sociopathic tendencies. Arthur told me that the good things people were quoted as saying about Richard were only because those people didn't know the man. Arthur felt that Richard was hiding his real self from others and that he was losing the ability to successfully continue to do that. My husband believed that Richard planned his disappearance because he feared being found out or that he would incriminate himself by being unable to keep up his façade."

"What did your husband think that Richard was hiding?" Angie's mind was racing and her heart pounded like a drum.

"Arthur didn't know, but he was sure that Richard ran away because of what he was hiding." Melinda's face hardened. "I hold Richard Connors partially responsible for my husband's death."

The four people around the table stared at the older woman who brushed at a tear threatening to escape from her eye.

"Arthur was consumed with worry. He could not stop thinking about Richard. I told him to pass his concerns over to the police. I was very, very worried about Arthur. His health was slipping, he had become frail. I was so worried that his fears about Richard would hurt him."

"Did telling the police about his worries help to

calm him at all?" Jenna asked.

Melinda shook her head slowly. "I came home one day from shopping and doing errands. There was a car in the driveway that I didn't know. When I came inside, Arthur was sitting here at the table with a woman and they were in the midst of a very serious discussion. I went into the kitchen to give them some privacy. After that conversation, Arthur had to go to bed. What little strength he had, had been drained from him. He didn't recover. He died two days later."

The sisters and Finch murmured sympathetic words.

Melinda's eyes glistened with tears. "The house is so quiet without my sweet Arthur in it." Brushing at her eyes, she added, "There is a hole in this house that will never be filled ... just like the hole in my heart."

Angie had to bite her lip to keep from tearing up. Mr. Finch gently placed his hand on top of Melinda's and said in a soft, kind voice, "We are truly sorry for your loss."

After a few minutes of silence, the group stood up and walked to the foyer, thanking Melinda for her time. They each hugged the woman and then headed for the front door, but just as Angie took a few steps in that direction, a wave of terrible unease clutched at her stomach with such force that she thought she might be sick. After taking in several deep breaths, the sensation that had overcome her eased and faded, but it left behind a slow, deep thrumming that pulsed through her blood.

Turning back to Melinda, Angie asked, even though she knew what the answer would be. "Who was the woman who was sitting with your husband at the dining table when you returned home that day?"

"It was Cora Connors. Arthur called her and asked that she come to speak with him."

"Arthur wanted to tell her that Richard was probably in Mill City?" Angie questioned.

"That, yes." Melinda's face was serious. "But he also wanted to warn her."

"Why?" Jenna asked. "About what?"

Melinda clasped her hands together. "Arthur wanted to talk to Mrs. Connors because he was sure she was in the path of terrible danger."

A cold of wave of fear washed down Angie's back.

CHAPTER 22

Mr. Finch entered the kitchen through the back door of the Victorian carrying a paper bag. Removing his winter coat and hanging it on the wall-hook, he joined Courtney at the kitchen island. "I made guacamole and salsa." The man took the bowls out of the bag and placed them on the counter. "Perhaps, they should be refrigerated before dinner. Miss Betty is unable to come for the meal, but she will join us later for games. She sent along her famous refried bean dip and chips."

Euclid sat next to Circe and trilled. The big orange boy loved Mexican food night at the Victorian. Mr. Finch winked up at the cats. "I agree with you, my friend."

Angie removed a pan of sopaipilla quesitos, cinnamon flavored pastries with a sweet, cream cheese filling, from the oven and set them aside to cool. Courtney was in the middle of preparing a veggie filling for tacos when Tom came in carrying his pan of home made enchiladas.

"What a feast we'll have." Mr. Finch's face was

beaming.

Ellie walked in from the hall. "Mr. Abel and Orla have accepted the invitation to dinner and game night. The other guests have plans and Cora declined." Ellie's eyebrow went up. "She wants to read." Gathering some linen napkins and some serving baskets, Ellie went to the dining room to set the table.

"To each, his own." Courtney slid the chopped veggies from the cutting board into a frying pan. "The others will miss a restaurant-quality meal."

"Not to mention the fine company." Finch smiled as he and Tom placed the Mexican beers into the refrigerator.

Jenna rushed in and hurried over to kiss Tom. "I've been working like crazy trying to get some jewelry orders out." She thanked Tom for bringing the enchiladas since she'd been too busy all day to contribute something to the meal. "I'll handle the clean-up since you've all been cooking." Sinking onto a stool, she made a face. "Those guests are driving me crazy."

"Who?" Courtney chuckled. "You mean the ones who have formed their very own Jenna Roseland fan club?"

Jenna rolled her eyes. "They came into the jewelry shop today. After an hour, I had to shoo them out or I wouldn't have gotten anything done."

Finch cocked his head. "You mean Mr. Abel and Ms. Orla?"

"They wouldn't stop asking me questions about the jewelry, where I went to school, how I come up with my designs, how Tom's and my house is coming along, when we're getting married, and on and on. It's exhausting. Really, it's mostly Orla who asks me all the questions. Mel just seems to tag along. Why doesn't she question all of you? It's just me."

Courtney laughed. "All Jenna, all the time. Maybe we could get you your own reality TV show."

"I find it unnerving." Jenna rubbed her forehead. "Please, please at dinner and during games tonight, deflect Orla's attention away from me."

"I'm on it, Sis." Courtney carried the frying pan to the stove.

Jenna shook her head. "And what about that other ID that Orla had in her wallet the night she checked in? Why does she have two IDs with two different names on them? What's up with that woman?"

"I don't think we'll figure that out unless we sneak into her room and look through her wallet." Courtney grinned. "And Ellie won't allow us to do that."

Angie was staring at her twin. "It is extremely odd that she is so interested in you."

"See," Jenna said to no one in particular. "Angie thinks it's weird, too."

Ellie came back into the kitchen. "Look who I

found." Chief Martin walked behind Ellie carrying a pan covered in tin foil. "Lucille made a creamy custard flan. She'll be here as soon as she gets out of work."

Tom handed the chief a beer just as Angie noted the look on the man's face. "What is it? You have some news, don't you?"

Chief Martin took a swallow from the bottle and then nodded his head. "I relayed the information to the Mill City police about the bill to Cora from the attorney." He glanced over his shoulder to make sure Cora wasn't about to enter the kitchen. "They looked into it. It seems that Cora visited the attorney to discuss divorce."

"What?" Jenna eyes were wide.

Courtney turned from the stove with a look of surprise, as shock registered on the other's faces.

"Divorce?" Angie's brow furrowed. "But Cora is always telling us that everything was fine between her and Richard."

"Mr. Abel was right." Courtney nodded. "He said we shouldn't trust Cora."

"Did the attorney share why Ms. Cora wanted to divorce her husband?" Finch looked to the chief.

Chief Martin sighed. "The attorney said that when Cora came to the meeting, she seemed extremely nervous and couldn't ... or *wouldn't* articulate her reasons for wanting a divorce. She only had that one meeting with the lawyer and never went back and never gave him the go-ahead to begin the proceedings."

"Cora isn't being up front with us." Angie was steaming. "How does she think we're going to find out anything helpful to this case if she holds back important information?"

"She claims to be upset that Richard disappeared." Jenna frowned. "Maybe she isn't so upset after all."

"She might have reason to be upset." The chief slid onto one of the kitchen island stools.

As all eyes focused on the chief, Euclid let out a low growl from his perch high up on top of the fridge.

Chief Martin glanced up at the cats. "Cora Connors may have reason to be upset about her husband. But the reason is not only because the man disappeared. The Mill City attorney told the police that he received a visit from a very angry man shortly after sending his bill to Cora."

"Richard?" Angie asked.

"Yes, Richard." The chief leaned forward, his elbows resting on the countertop. "Richard demanded to know why Cora had a meeting with the attorney. He wanted to know what they talked about. After the attorney explained client confidentiality, he was sure that Richard was going to strike him. Richard ranted about how he didn't care about confidentiality rules. He wanted to know what his wife was up to. The attorney lifted his telephone and was about to call the police when

Richard decided he'd better leave the lawyer's office."

"Wow. What was that all about?" Courtney shook her head. "Why did Cora think about filing for divorce?"

The chief continued. "The attorney said that as Richard was leaving the office, he was muttering things like *what is she up to?, is she trying to find out about me?*, things like that. The attorney was sure that Richard Connors was unbalanced."

A voice was heard coming from the back of the kitchen. "I agree. Things about Mr. Connors are not adding up."

Everyone turned to see Jack Ford standing just inside the rear hall removing his coat. "I need to tell all of you some things having to do with Richard Connors."

***

The family and Chief Martin gathered around Jack to hear what he had to say.

"As you know, Mrs. Connors retained me to look into whether or not Richard's credit card had been compromised. I, too, am bound by client confidentiality, but seeing that Chief Martin is here and is assisting the Mill City police, I will tell you that it does not seem to be the case that someone has stolen or found Mr. Connors's credit card. There have been only the two charges made in New

183

Hampshire for some clothing and the motel room. When a card is compromised, the guilty party usually makes quite a few charges in a very short period of time knowing that the card will be reported stolen. It's usually a case of hit and run, buy and charge up a storm, sometimes within hours, in order to get as much purchased as possible before the credit card is cancelled." Jack looked from one person to the other. "I think that the card was used by Richard Connors."

"Have you told Cora what you think?" Angie asked.

"I have." Jack nodded. "I thought she would be pleased that her husband is probably alive, but she didn't react that way."

"How *did* she react?" Ellie stood off to the side listening to Jack's information.

"Visibly upset, nervous. She tried to explain her reaction as being shocked and happy, but I wasn't buying it." Jack adjusted his red and black bow tie. "My report to her about the credit card was *not* what she wanted to hear."

"I wonder if Richard threatened Cora after he found out that she went to see the lawyer?" Ellie nervously twisted a lock of her long hair.

Courtney kept her voice low. "Maybe Cora wanted to get rid of Richard. Maybe divorce wasn't enough. Did Cora hire someone to do something to Richard, to get rid of him permanently?" Her voice was tinged with the excitement of a possible answer to their questions. "Maybe whoever she hired messed up and Richard killed that guy." She paused for a moment. "And now Richard is back to take revenge on Cora."

"Yikes." Ellie moved over to stand next to Jack.

Anxiety squeezed Angie's throat and she reached for Tom's beer bottle to take a swallow from it. "Ugh. This is a mess."

"What are we going to do?" Jenna squeezed Tom's hand.

"We'd better have a talk with Cora." Chief Martin pulled his cell phone out of his pocket and headed for the back hall. "I'm going to call the Mill City detective that I know. Would you go ask Cora to come down and speak with me?"

Angie nodded and headed for the foyer to go up to Cora's room. She knocked several times, but no one came to the door. As she turned away from the woman's room, Mel Abel stepped from his suite into the hall and spotted Angie.

"You looking for Cora?" Mel's voice boomed even though he was only a few yards from Angie.

Angie nodded. "Have you seen her?"

"Yeah, she took off a few minutes ago. I saw her go out the front door. You just missed her."

Angie groaned as little sparks of anxiety jumped down her spine.

CHAPTER 23

The Mexican dinner night was a hit with fourteen people gathered around the table enjoying the delicious food and the pleasant chatter. Even Mel Abel's voice didn't seem quite so loud mixed in with the din of everyone else's conversations. After the meal was finished, game night began with part of the group moving into the living room for several rounds of charades while the others sat around the dining table playing cards and board games. Rufus Fudge and Mel Abel had a friendly rivalry going over cards and the air was punctuated every few minutes with hoots and groans and laughter as Betty Hayes, Jack, and Tom tried their best to outdo the two card sharks.

Despite the fun and levity, a number of the players were distracted thinking about Cora Connors and the revelation that she had inquired about filing for divorce from her husband shortly before Richard went missing. They also wondered where Cora had gone off to and what she would have to say when the chief questioned her about considering a divorce from her husband. Angie kept glancing to the front door hoping the woman would return.

It was after 11pm when the boyfriends began to gather their things, Betty and Mr. Finch headed for her car so she could drive him home, and Orla and Mel climbed the staircase to their rooms.

"I'm thinking of moving in here permanently," Mel joked when he was half-way up the stairs. "I've never met a finer group of people."

The four Roseland sisters smiled, but shuddered slightly, imagining Mel Abel shouting all day every day in the Victorian.

As Chief Martin and his wife started for the front door, they thanked the sisters for a lovely evening. "I'll be back tomorrow for a chat with Mrs. Connors," the chief said. "Would you tell her I'm coming by?"

When quiet returned and everything had been put away, the girls headed for the family room with the two cats following behind.

"So where did Cora go off to?" Courtney sat in her usual seat with Euclid positioned on his stomach over her lap with his head hanging down one side and his legs and tail draped over the other.

"She's gone off before," Ellie noted. "She's gone home to get clothes and pick up mail. I guess she doesn't trust Karl to handle bringing in some envelopes from the mailbox."

Jenna scratched Circe's cheeks. "It seemed a

coincidence that Cora left right before Chief Martin was about to talk to her. She couldn't have heard us talking about her." Jenna made a face. "Could she?"

"No." Angie shook her head. "At least I don't think she could have."

"It doesn't matter if she did or not." Courtney wanted to get her sisters back on track. "A divorce, huh. Cora hasn't given us any hint that she was considering divorce. I would call that withholding pertinent information from us."

Jenna pulled a cashmere throw blanket over her legs. "Richard confronted the lawyer that Cora went to. The lawyer described Richard's behavior as threatening. The lawyer must have mentioned this to Cora, yet she doesn't think that would be something to share with us?"

Courtney grunted. "Mel Abel was right. We shouldn't trust a thing she says to us."

Ellie pulled her legs up under herself. "Let's think about this. Why wouldn't Cora tell us those things? Why would she want to hide it?"

Angie shrugged. "Maybe she's trying to paint a picture for us of their perfect family life. Maybe she got fed up over something, went to the lawyer, and then decided she'd made more of it than she should have. Maybe she's embarrassed that she flew off the handle over something minor."

Ellie frowned. "Then Richard flies off the handle because Cora went to a lawyer? How have those two stayed married for over twenty years if they both overreact about things?"

The four sat thinking about the situation.

Jenna spoke up. "Trying to make their family seem perfect is a dumb thing to do. No one is perfect."

Courtney smiled. "Except us."

Euclid looked up at her and trilled.

Jenna ignored her youngest sister. "Not only is pretending that everything is wonderful *not* helpful, but telling us things like that can throw us off the path completely. Does Cora want this thing solved or not? Is it more important to her that everyone thinks the family is something that they're not or that the case gets solved?"

Something pinged in Angie's brain and she turned and looked at Jenna so suddenly that the others stared at her.

"What?" Jenna eyed Angie.

"What you said. Just now. *Something they're not.*" Angie jumped to her feet. "It could explain it. Why didn't I think of this before? Jenna, the laptop."

The three sisters narrowed their eyes at Angie. Euclid slowly got to his feet and turned towards the young woman. He flicked his tail back and forth and let out a low growl.

Jenna stood up. "What is it?"

"Where was Richard Connors born?" Angie looked from sister to sister. "Does anyone remember?"

"Um. Massachusetts?" Courtney offered.

"No," Ellie said. "He was mostly in foster homes in Massachusetts. He and his mother moved all around New England. I don't recall where he was born, but it wasn't Massachusetts."

"I have the case notes right here on the desk." Jenna sat down in the desk chair and opened the folder they had been keeping about the disappearance. "I should have remembered this. It says that Richard was born in South Carolina."

"That's it. Go online." Angie's eyes were wide and her heart was pounding. "Go to the South Carolina vital records database. Search for a copy of his birth certificate." By using his age, Angie calculated the year that Richard was born and told Jenna what it was.

Jenna tapped away. "I didn't know that just anyone could look up and request a copy of someone's birth certificate."

Excitement pulsed down Angie's back as she leaned over Jenna's shoulder. "What does it say? What are his parent's names?"

"Hold on." Jenna leaned closer to the screen and tapped at the keyboard.

"What's going on? Why are you doing this?" Courtney walked over to the desk.

"I'm not going to say anything until I see what comes up." Angie was holding her breath hoping that her idea would be correct.

Jenna leaned back. "I either need the exact date that Richard was born or I need the city or town where he was born."

"Okay." Angie looked at Ellie. "Will you call Jack? Ask him to come back here."

"It's almost midnight." Ellie looked dumbfounded.

"Jack won't mind." Angie took a pen and a pad of paper off the desk and went to sit on the sofa. "He loves intrigue."

Ellie frowned, but made the call to her boyfriend. When she clicked off, she said, "He'll be here in five minutes."

Courtney and Jenna sat down on either side of Angie.

"Now tell us what's going on." Courtney watched as Angie jotted some notes.

"I think it's identity theft." Angie didn't look up from the paper.

"But Jack told us that no one stole Richard's credit card." Jenna's brows scrunched together. "He thinks that Richard used the card himself."

"It's not the credit card," Angie said. "It's Richard."

Her three sisters stared at her blankly.

Angie looked up. "Richard. I don't think that's his real name. I think he's assumed someone's identity. I bet he did it in his late teens or early twenties. A long time ago, I read an article about someone doing that very thing. I can't recall the particulars, but I remember thinking that it was amazingly simple to do. There were a number of steps, done in different states, but the person successfully changed her identity."

Ellie narrowed her eyes. "It makes sense. It must be why I've been thinking that Richard isn't who he says he is. I didn't understand my feeling, but now it makes perfect sense."

"Wow." Courtney was amazed that changing identity could be done without getting caught. "I should know all this stuff from the crime shows we watch." She smiled. "Wait until we tell Mr. Finch about this."

Ellie's phone buzzed with a text from Jack saying he was at the front door and didn't want to ring the bell in case it woke the guests. She hurried to get him and returned to the family room with Jack in tow. Despite the late hour, Jack was still wearing his bow tie.

Courtney kidded him. "Do you wear a bow tie to bed at night?"

Jack looked at the youngest Roseland sister and deadpanned. "Yes."

When they were settled on chairs and sofas, Angie explained her thoughts that Richard had assumed an identity.

Jack listened intently and nodded now and then. "Yes. It's more common than you'd think. It's certainly possible that Richard has done this."

Jenna said, "I bet this is why Richard blew a

gasket when he found out that Cora visited an attorney. I bet he was afraid that his cover would be blown and that Cora and the authorities would find out who he really is. Maybe he committed a crime and he's afraid that he'll be found out."

Jack borrowed the pen and paper from Angie and wrote a few notes. "I'll start looking into it in the morning. If Richard Connors has indeed assumed someone's identity, then there must be a reason for doing so. And that reason probably isn't a good one."

Angie's heart skipped a beat. "If he went to all that trouble to change who he is, then I bet what he's hiding in his past is pretty darned bad."

Ellie took in a deep breath. "And I bet he thinks Cora knows what he's hiding."

They all looked at each other with wide eyes and worried faces wondering what lengths Richard Connors might go to in order to keep his secret a secret.

CHAPTER 24

Business in the bake shop had been busier that usual and Angie and Louisa were like blurs hurrying from one customer to another, and the young women removed batter from the refrigerator that Angie had made that morning and placed tins of muffins to bake in the two commercial ovens so that they wouldn't run out.

The day was overcast with heavy cloud cover and during a lull in the morning rush, Angie went out to the porch to add some long white birch branches to the two decorative pots that stood on each side of the bake shop door and she could feel the moisture in the air foretelling of a coming storm.

"Here's a sight for my sore eyes." Josh Williams came up the steps to the porch with a huge smile on his face and wrapped his arms around Angie. "I'm headed up to Portsmouth for a meeting and decided to stop into the bake shop to fortify me for the drive."

"You need some black coffee and a muffin to take along?" Angie smiled up at her sweetheart.

"No. I needed to see you." Josh winked. "Last night was great. I need to improve my card-playing skills so that I can beat Rufus one of these days."

Angie chuckled as she held Josh's hand and led him into the bake shop. "It might take you a lot of practice if that's your goal."

"Did you hear the weather report? There's a big snowstorm coming tonight. I need to get back from Portsmouth before it starts."

"Louisa told me that the prediction is for ten inches of snow." Angie shook her head. "Maybe it will blow out to sea."

Josh took a seat on the stool at the counter while Angie prepared his take-out coffee and a box of pastries to take on his drive up the coast. When she set the cup in front of Josh and snapped on the lid, she leaned forward and spoke softly telling him what they thought about the possibility that Richard Connors had assumed an identity. "Jack is going to start researching it this morning."

Josh's eyes clouded. "I don't like this. This guy is probably dangerous. I wish Mrs. Connors wasn't staying here at the B and B. I don't want them bringing trouble to your home."

Angie leaned across the counter. "Chief Martin wanted to talk to Cora last evening, but she'd gone out. She hadn't returned by the time we all went to bed, which was late. Ellie knocked on her door this morning and she didn't answer. Either she didn't return at all last night or she left the Victorian very early this morning. The chief wants us to call him as soon as Cora shows up."

"Maybe she isn't coming back. Maybe she's gone home?" Josh's voice held a hopeful tone.

Angie shook her head. "She hasn't checked out. She didn't leave the key."

Worry lines etched into Josh's forehead as he looked into Angie's eyes and reached for her hand. "Be careful."

Ellie stepped into the bake shop from the Victorian's connecting kitchen. She greeted Josh and then turned to Angie. "Are you still going to the market when you close up for the day?"

Angie nodded as she packed a box of homemade donuts for a customer. "Want me to pick up some things for you?"

"Could you?" Ellie handed Angie a list of items. "I don't want to run out of anything in case that storm hits."

Josh stood up and leaned forward to kiss Angie. "I'd better get going. If the snow starts early, I don't want to be on the highway in the dark with cars sliding all around."

"Call me when you get back." Angie smiled at the handsome man.

The rest of the work day went by in a flash as Angie and Louisa waited on the regular lunch crowd and the tourists who stopped by on their way north for skiing or heading south to other seacoast towns or to the Boston area. Everyone's chatter was focused on the coming storm and whether or not it might reach blizzard proportions.

Ever sense Josh had left for his business trip, a sense of unease and apprehension flooded Angie's body and she felt distracted and on edge as she went about the end of the day tasks in the bake shop.

After locking up, she pulled her apron over her head as she walked into the Victorian's kitchen. She wanted to shower and change before borrowing Jenna's car and heading to the market. Angie smiled thinking about the chaos she would encounter in the grocery store as everyone flooded the place in a panic over the storm about to hit.

Ellie was standing at the counter cutting up fruit to make a fruit salad for the guests.

"Any sign of Cora?" Angie headed for the hallway.

"Nothing. Where did that woman go?" Ellie grumped. "Jenna and Courtney went to Jenna's house to do more painting and Mr. Finch is at the candy store. Are you coming right home after the market? I've been feeling odd ever since last night."

Angie eyed her sister.

"I feel sort of nervous and on edge." Ellie sliced several oranges into pieces.

The two sisters made eye contact and sensations of worry jumped between them.

"Have you heard anything from Jack," Angie asked.

"Not yet."

Angie gave Ellie a slight nod. "I'll be back as soon as I get the groceries." As she stepped into the hallway, she attempted a reassuring tone. "The cats are here with you."

Ellie glanced up to the top of the fridge where Euclid and Circe sat at attention. "Thank heavens," she muttered. "Don't leave me, you two."

***

Ellie stood in the dining room placing the carafes of tea and coffee on the buffet table when Cora, bundled in a bulky winter coat, walked into the room from the hallway startling Ellie and causing her to whirl around.

"Oh, you're back. I didn't hear you come in."

"I just got back." Cora brushed some snow flakes from her coat. "I parked at the end of the driveway and came in through the back door."

"Did you go home?" Ellie asked.

Cora nodded. "I needed to get some things. It's starting to snow already."

"Is it?" Ellie bent down to look out the window.

"Not hard yet, just flurries." Cora set her small suitcase on the floor. "I'm going to leave my bag here for a minute. I've got some other things I want to get from the car."

Ellie called after the woman. "Chief Martin would like to speak with you. He'd like you to give him a call."

Cora looked over her shoulder with an expression of apprehension on her face. "Okay."

Ellie headed back to the buffet table when the front doorbell rang and she went to open it. A tall man in a black winter coat and a woolen hat pulled over his hair stood on the porch. "Hello. I wondered if you have a room for the night. I'd like to get off the roads with the storm starting."

Ellie stepped back to let the man into the foyer and as she did, a wave of anxiety washed over with such force that she almost lost her balance. The man closed the front door after him and turned around to see Euclid and Circe standing in the foyer a few yards away, their backs arched and their green eyes practically glowing. Ellie backed into the dining room, her heart in her throat.

"I'm mistaken. We don't have any available rooms." Ellie's voice shook.

The man's face hardened. "That's okay. I'm really just looking for someone. I'd like to speak to one of your guests. Cora Connors."

Ellie heard footsteps in the hall behind her. Keeping her eyes on the man near the front door, she called out without looking back. "Stay back there, Cora. Don't come out here."

It was too late. Cora stood three feet behind Ellie.

"Hello, Richard." Cora's voice was weak.

Ellie's heart was in her throat as she whispered

to the woman standing at her back. "Get out of here. Go."

Cora hesitated, but Ellie shoved her. "Go!"

As Cora rushed down the hall, Euclid advanced several steps towards the man, moving in a threatening sideways motion, his back arched.

Richard's hand moved to take something from his jacket pocket and was about to lunge in Ellie's direction, when she held up her hands, palms facing the man, her eyes closed and her long blonde hair rising up to float around her head.

Before Richard could take two steps, objects from the dining room and the foyer table shot into the air like cannon balls and pummeled the man in the head.

Richard reached up flailing to protect himself, stumbled, and fell to the floor. Scrambling up, he stared at Ellie while thrashing his arms about trying to strike at the objects hurtling towards him, and with a look of horror, he half-crawled, half-ran to the front door. Flinging it open, he tumbled out onto the porch just as Euclid and Circe flew like orange and black missiles and plunged their front claws into the back of the man's head and neck.

Mel Abel, Mr. Finch, and Angie, holding grocery bags in their arms, stood at the bottom of the porch steps gaping at the howling man writhing before them.

Ellie screeched from inside. "Don't let him get away!"

Mel's hands released the bags and let them fall to the ground as he hustled up the three stairs and plopped heavily down on top of Richard. Looking back at Angie with a grin, Mel bellowed. "Sometimes it comes in handy to be the size and shape of a nearly three hundred pound pumpkin."

Angie couldn't help but return Mel's smile as she pulled out her phone and called the police. Mr. Finch pulled himself up the stairs holding his cane at the ready in case Connors tried to free himself from Mel's custody. Leaning down Finch patted the two cats and praised them for helping to subdue the suspect. "We have many ways available to protect ourselves and our friends." He grinned. "Unorthodox as they may be."

Ellie, drained from using her telekinesis to stop Richard Connors and feeling like she was about to faint, gripped the foyer table trying to steady herself. Something at the top of the stairs caught her eye and she glanced up to see Orla on the second floor landing leaning over the railing, staring down at her.

Orla's short, auburn curls bounced around her face as she nodded and smiled. "Nice work."

The color drained from Ellie's face, horrified that someone had seen what she'd just done.

Orla winked as she turned to go back to her room. "I only helped you a little."

CHAPTER 25

Richard Connors was taken into custody and several days later Chief Martin arrived at the Victorian to tell the Roselands, Mr. Finch, and the two cats the strange story of the man's past.

The chief rubbed his forehead as everyone gathered in the family room to hear the tale. "Richard Connors, real name Matt Brown, murdered a young woman in Rhode Island when he was eighteen and living in that state briefly on his own. Richard, as we know him, remembered hearing as a kid about a house fire in South Carolina that killed a family including their two-year-old son, Mitchell Waters. Richard, then named Matt, ordered the little boy's birth certificate and took it to Ohio where he obtained a state identification card using the birth certificate as his own. Now he had a picture ID with the name Mitchell Waters on it. Next stop was West Virginia where he picked up a driver's license using that name.

"This is unbelievable." Ellie shook her head.

The chief went on with the story. "About five years later, he moved to Nevada where he petitioned the court to change his name from Mitchell Waters to Richard Connors. The petition was granted. Richard used the court paperwork to request a new social security card using his new name ... and his transformation was complete."

"This is possible?" Angie was dumbfounded. "I can't believe it."

Chief Martin shook his head and shrugged. "A clever bunch of actions. Richard worked for a while and obtained a GED diploma. He moved to Mill City and enrolled in the state university there where he met Cora."

"No wonder Richard freaked out when he discovered that Cora had been to an attorney. He must have been scared to death that the lawyer would find some information about his past." Courtney looked at Mr. Finch. "This should be made into an episode of the true crime show we watch."

Finch's face was sad. "A terrible story. From what we've heard, Richard Connors must be older than he claims to be."

"Yes," the chief said. "Mr. Connors is probably about ten years older than he purports to be."

"His mother-in-law was right," Jenna observed. "She told us she was sure that Richard was *not* one year older than Cora. She was sure he was several years older than he claimed to be."

"His mother-in-law was right." Finch adjusted his glass frames. "So the man ran off and left his family because he was afraid that his past might be discovered."

Chief Martin let out a sigh. "Richard had fake IDs and a secret bank account, all obtained a few years ago in case he had to flee."

"Yikes." Jenna just shook her head. The whole story was like some crazy television movie. "He came back to hurt Cora?"

"It seems so. Mr. Connors doesn't seem to be thinking clearly. He confessed that he wanted to kill Cora to keep her from revealing her concerns about his past. The mess of his life has taken a severe toll on the man. He is being evaluated by a team of doctors and psychiatrists."

Courtney frowned. "Things might have been easier for all of us if Cora had shared her concerns about her husband."

Cora revealed to police that she had harbored suspicions about her husband's past for years and became alarmed recently when her husband's mood and personality took a turn for the worse. He had become verbally abusive to her and she feared that whatever Richard might have been hiding was about to explode. Hoping that her worries were unfounded, she kept her suspicions to herself.

Chief Martin looked over at Ellie and the cats. "My thanks to the three of you. I believe that it was very fortunate that Cora was here at the inn when

Mr. Connors found her. Otherwise ...."

Euclid puffed up his chest at the chief's words of thanks and Circe let out a trill.

Ellie's cheeks tinged pink. The tall blonde had admitted to everyone that she was tired of being a wimp and had decided to secretly practice and hone her telekinesis skills in case she ever needed to defend her family and friends. "I think that our guest, Orla O'Brien, deserves some of the credit for stopping Richard Connors."

As it turned out, Orla O'Brien was staying at the B and B in order to obtain the necklace that had been the cause of the carriage house fire in the fall. Orla's mission with the necklace was not revealed to the sisters, but she did tell them that she traveled the world for "special" reasons and used different IDs and credit cards to keep her identity a secret. "It was quite careless of me to let the other license slip from my wallet that evening," she'd told the family.

Because Jenna was a jewelry designer, Orla was sure that she was the "keeper" of the necklace and that was the reason why Orla was always questioning the young woman.

Orla had sighed. "Perhaps, it's time I retired." When she told this to the sisters and Finch, Orla looked at Ellie. "You might like this job. Shall I recommend you to replace me?" When Ellie heard that offer, she practically fainted and Orla took that as a no.

Ellie took Orla into her office, opened the safe, removed the necklace in its special lead case, and gently placed the box in Orla's hands. Even though Ellie couldn't wait for someone to come to collect the necklace from her and take it away, several tears rolled down her cheeks as Orla tucked the box into her carry-on case.

The next morning Orla was packed and ready to go and as she said her goodbyes to the family, Mel Abel ambled down the staircase carrying his suitcase.

"I'm ready to go," he boomed, a broad smile across his face. He and Orla beamed at each other.

The sisters and Mr. Finch looked from Orla to Mel with surprised expressions.

"Mel and I have decided to travel together." Orla blushed. "We're tired of being alone."

Mel wrapped his meaty arms around each sister in a bear hug and shook Mr. Finch's hand with vigor. "And guess what? Orla and I will be returning to the B and B in the spring. Orla will be retiring and we just love this little town." Mel winked. "Not to mention the fine people in it. We're going to buy a house here."

Jenna smiled. "Then you'll be here for Tom's and my wedding. We've finally picked the day." She told them the date of the May wedding and Orla and Mel said they wouldn't miss it.

"Goodbye for now." The two people were heading down the steps of the porch when Mel looked back to Courtney. "Tell that young Englishman of yours that when I return, I will whip his fanny at our next card game."

***

On the night that Richard Connors was taken away by the police, Mother Nature dumped over ten inches of snow on the quiet town of Sweet Cove turning the already beautiful haven into a glistening winter wonderland. The following Saturday afternoon, the sisters and their boyfriends and Mr. Finch and Betty bundled up and headed to the big hill behind the town common with snow sleds and toboggans.

Everyone roared with laughter when Betty, screaming with delight, hurtled down the snow-covered hill with Mr. Finch hunched behind her on the sled, his arms clutched tightly around her waist.

Tom pulled the sled up the hill with Mr. Finch sitting on it as Betty trudged through the snow beside them and when they reached the top, everyone cheered and applauded.

Finch's cheeks were rosy red and his eyes danced with joy. "It is most exhilarating!" he shouted in a breathless voice.

Watching their humans from the front seats of Ellie's van, Euclid and Circe trilled at their family's happy antics.

Soon everyone was racing each other down the

hill and the crisp, cold air rang with laughter and whoops of glee. A playful snowball fight started at the bottom of the hill and by the end of the afternoon, each person was covered in snow from head to toe.

As the car was being loaded up to head back to the Victorian for hot chocolate and slices of cake, Angie plopped backwards in the snow and flailed her arms and legs side to side to make a snow angel. Resting on her back for a moment, she stared up at the bright blue sky and watched the perfect white puffs of clouds gracefully floating overhead. Thinking about how lucky she was, Angie sighed contentedly and her heart flooded with warmth.

Josh called from beside Ellie's van. "Come on, Angie. We're ready."

Angie stood up and crunched over the sparkling snow to the van where Josh stood waiting for his sweetheart with a beaming smile and love shining in his eyes.

And all was right with the world ... for now.

THANK YOU FOR READING!

BOOKS BY J.A. WHITING CAN BE FOUND HERE:

www.amazon.com/author/jawhiting

To hear about new books and book sales, please sign up for my mailing list at:

www.jawhitingbooks.com

Your email will never be sold, shared, or spammed.

SWEET COVE COZY MYSTERIES

The Sweet Dreams Bake Shop (Sweet Cove Cozy Mystery Book 1)
Murder So Sweet (Sweet Cove Cozy Mystery Book 2)
Sweet Secrets (Sweet Cove Cozy Mystery Book 3)
Sweet Deceit (Sweet Cove Cozy Mystery Book 4)
Sweetness and Light (Sweet Cove Cozy Mystery

Book 5)

Home Sweet Home (Sweet Cove Cozy Mystery Book 6)

Sweet Fire and Stone (Sweet Cove Cozy Mystery Book 7)

Sweet Friend of Mine (Sweet Cove Cozy Mystery Book 8)

Sweet Hide and Seek (Sweet Cove Cozy Mystery Book 9)

And more to come!

LIN COFFIN COZY MYSTERIES

A Haunted Murder (A Lin Coffin Cozy Mystery Book 1)

A Haunted Disappearance (A Lin Coffin Cozy Mystery Book 2)

The Haunted Bones (A Lin Coffin Cozy Mystery Book 3)

A Haunted Theft (A Lin Coffin Cozy Mystery Book 4)

A Haunted Invitation (A Lin Coffin Cozy Mystery Book 5)

A Haunted Lighthouse (A Lin Coffin Cozy Mystery Book 6)

And more to come!

MYSTERIES

The Killings (Olivia Miller Mystery – Book 1)

Sweet Hide and Seek

Red Julie (Olivia Miller Mystery - Book 2)
The Stone of Sadness (Olivia Miller Mystery - Book 3)

If you enjoyed the book, please consider leaving a review.

A few words are all that's needed.

It would be very much appreciated.

ABOUT THE AUTHOR

J.A. Whiting lives with her family in New England where she works full time in education. Whiting loves reading and writing mystery and suspense stories.

VISIT ME AT:

www.jawhitingbooks.com

www.facebook.com/jawhitingauthor

www.amazon.com/author/jawhiting

SOME RECIPES FROM THE SWEET COVE SERIES

CHOCOLATE PUDDING CAKE

Ingredients

¾ cup all-purpose flour
1½ teaspoons baking powder
½ cup sugar
½ cup unsweetened cocoa powder
½ teaspoon salt
½ cup milk (2 percent or whole)
2-3 Tablespoons vegetable oil
½ cup packed brown sugar
¼ cup of mini semisweet chocolate chips
1½ teaspoons vanilla extract
1⅓ cup hot water

Directions

Heat oven to 350°F.

In a mixing bowl, mix together flour, sugar, ¼ cup of the cocoa, baking powder, and salt.

Add milk and oil and mix well.

Pour the mixture into a 8 X 8 square pan.

Sprinkle the brown sugar, the rest of the cocoa, and the chocolate chips over the top.

Add vanilla to the hot water.

Gently pour the hot water over the top of the mixture.

Bake for 30-35 minutes in the preheated oven.

Remove from the oven when the top of the mixture looks dry.

Serve with ice cream or whipped cream!

HONEY CAKE

Ingredients

½ - ¾ cup honey
8 ounces unsalted butter
1/4 cup sugar
3 large eggs, beaten
¾ cup of self-raising flour

Directions

Heat oven to 325°F.

Grease and line (parchment paper) an 8 inch round springform cake pan.

Cut the butter into pieces.

In a medium saucepan, place the butter, sugar, and honey. Melt slowly over low heat. When the ingredients have turned to liquid, increase the heat and boil the mixture for about one minute.

Cool the mixture for 20 minutes.

Using a fork, beat the eggs into the melted honey mixture.

Place the flour into a bowl and pour in the egg and honey mixture. Beat with the fork until the mixture is smooth and runny.

Pour the mixture into the prepared cake pan.

Bake for 40-50 minutes until golden and a toothpick inserted into the center comes out clean.

Optional: Warm 2-4 Tablespoons of honey in a saucepan. Brush over the top of the cake.

Cool.

BLUEBERRY CRUMBLE CAKE

Ingredients

1 16 ounce package of frozen blueberries
or 4 cups of fresh blueberries
2½ Tablespoons lemon juice
¾ cup light brown sugar
2 teaspoons corn starch
¾ cup quick-cook oats
½ cup all-purpose flour
pinch of salt
⅓ cup butter, cut into pieces

Directions

Heat oven to 350°F.

Toss the blueberries with the lemon juice and place in a 1½ quart casserole dish.

Mix ¼ cup of the brown sugar with the cornstarch. Mix into the blueberries.

Mix oats, ½ cup of the brown sugar, flour, and salt until well combined.

With a fork, cut the butter into the oats mixture. Sprinkle the mixture over the blueberries.

Bake until the topping is light brown and blueberries bubble (about 35-40 minutes).

Serve with ice cream or whipped cream.

EASY SOPAIPILLA CREAM CHEESE SQUARES

Ingredients

2 8-ounce containers of Pillsbury crescent rolls
2 8-ounce packages of cream cheese (room temperature)
¾ cup sugar
1 teaspoon vanilla
¼ cup melted butter
2 Tablespoons cinnamon
½ teaspoon nutmeg
4 tablespoons sugar

Directions

Heat oven to 350°F.

Spray a 9 X 13 inch baking dish with cooking spray.

Open a can of crescent rolls and lightly press them into the bottom of the baking dish. Pinch edges together so there are no spaces.

Bake this first layer in the oven for 5 minutes.

Combine softened cream cheese, ¾ cup of sugar, and vanilla.

Spread the mixture over the crescent rolls.

Open the second container of crescent rolls and lay them over the top of the mixture. Gently stretch the layer of rolls to the edges of the pan and seal.

Brush the top with the melted butter.
Mix together the cinnamon, nutmeg, and sugar and sprinkle evenly over the top of the rolls.

Bake for 30 minutes until golden in color.

Chill for 1-2 hours.

Slice into bars.

CREAMY CARAMEL FLAN

Ingredients

1 cup sugar
½ cup water
¼ teaspoon of lemon juice
1 8-ounce package of cream cheese, softened
5 large eggs
1 can (about 14 ounces) condensed milk
1 can (about 12 ounces) evaporated milk
1½ teaspoons vanilla extract

Directions

In a heavy saucepan, on medium-high heat, constantly stir sugar and water with a wooden spoon until melted.

When melted, add the lemon juice and stir.

Bring the mixture to a boil, then lower the heat to medium and stop stirring.

Simmer for about 10 minutes. Watch the color carefully — it will turn to golden and then to amber very quickly! Remove from the heat as soon as it turns an amber color.

Quickly pour the melted sugar mixture into a 2 quart round baking dish. Tilt the dish so that the sugar swirls around and coats the bottom. Let stand for about 10 minutes.

In a bowl, beat the cream cheese until smooth.

Beat in the eggs, one at a time.

Add the rest of the ingredients and mix well.

Pour over the caramelized sugar in the baking dish.

Place the baking dish into a larger baking pan. Pour boiling water into the outer baking pan to create a depth of about 1 inch.

Bake at 350 degrees for about 50 minutes or until the center looks set. The mixture will jiggle.

Remove the baking dish to a wire rack and cool for 1 hour.

Place in the refrigerator over night.

When ready to remove the flan from the pan –
Run a knife gently around the edges of the pan.
Invert onto a serving platter.
Cut into wedges and serve.

VEGGIE AND LENTIL BOLOGNESE

Ingredients

1 Tablespoon olive oil
1 large onion, finely chopped
2 carrots, chopped into small cubes
1 sweet potato, chopped into small cubes
1½ cups of sliced mushrooms
2-3 garlic cloves, crushed
1 cup lentils (any color)
15-ounce can of chopped tomatoes
1 cup of vegetable stock
3 Tablespoons tomato paste
2 Tablespoons apple cider vinegar
½ cup red wine (if you prefer, you may substitute water)
1 teaspoon dried basil
1 teaspoon rosemary

Directions

Chop the vegetables as noted above.

Heat the oil in a frying pan on low.

Saute the onions, garlic, carrots, sweet potato, and mushrooms until softened.

Add the rest of the ingredients and simmer for 25 minutes until sauce has thickened.

Serve over pasta and sprinkle with cheese of your choice.

Made in the USA
Coppell, TX
30 August 2020

35649470R00135